D1527871

For All the
Wrong Reasons

By Mary Lydon Simonsen

Quail Creek Publishing, LLC

This story was previously published on fan fiction websites and my blog. However, many changes have been made since it first appeared in 2010, and it is no longer available on line.

Printed in the United States of America
Published by Quail Creek Publishing, LLC
quailcreekpub@hotmail.com
www.marysimonsenfanfiction.blogspot.com
ISBN: 1461010128
ISBN-13: 978-1461010128

©2011 Quail Creek Publishing LLC

Cover artwork is an illustration by Charles E. Brock of Jane Austen's *Pride and Prejudice*, circa 1900.

Chapter 1

As Darcy paced, Georgiana watched. It was the young Miss Darcy's letter that had triggered everything. When she posted the letter to her brother at Netherfield Park, she had placed no particular importance on anything contained within its pages. It was merely a summary of the latest news being circulated around town, including a one-line item in a gossip sheet that she thought would amuse her brother: *Caroline Bingley to wed Peter Grayson*. But Will's reaction had been immediate and dramatic. Two days later he arrived in town with Charles Bingley in tow. Poor Mr. Bingley, equally surprised by the turn of events, had set out for London for the purpose of finding out the truth of the matter.

Weeks earlier, Caroline and Louisa had returned to London from Hertfordshire. Because of their brother's marriage to Miss Jane Bennet, there was no reason for them to remain in the country as Jane was now mistress of Netherfield Park. In addition to Caroline's intense dislike of Jane's relations, there was another reason for her departure. She had finally come to the realization that she was never going to secure Mr. Darcy, and in her unhappiness, she had told Charles that she felt ill used by that gentleman. If he had had no interest in her, then why had he remained at their country house, week after week after week, for two months? And how was one to account for the many comments he had made about her accomplishments? Why had he complimented her on her proficiency on the pianoforte, her exquisite needlework, and her fine voice? Why bother saying anything if he had no intention of initiating a courtship?

Charles had attempted to rebut his sister's arguments. In the first place, Darcy had come to Hertfordshire at *his* invitation. It was Caroline who had insisted that she was needed at Netherfield Park, stating that someone must keep house for him. When he had explained that his primary purpose in coming to the country was to ride and shoot, *she* had pressed the issue. Although it was true that Darcy had praised her on several occasions, he had also paid Louisa a fair amount of compliments, and she had to admit that Darcy had a reputation for acknowledging talent wherever he found it, young or old, male or female, regardless of social standing. It was *she* who had attached romantic significance to his remarks about her accomplishments.

But Charles could just as easily have been talking to the dog as Caroline had refused to hear any defense of his friend, and after crying buckets of tears, she had removed to London in a huff with barely a parting word to her new sister-in-law and with "a heart full of rancor."

"You know nothing of this matter?" Darcy again asked Georgiana. "While I was in Hertfordshire, Peter did not call or write or somehow indicate that he was courting Miss Bingley?"

"Will, I have told you everything I know," an exhausted Georgiana answered. She had no idea that one sentence in a letter would result in an inquisition being launched by her brother. "As I have already mentioned twice, my good friend, Alice Montague, lives three houses down from the Bingleys. It was she who told me that Peter Grayson had become something of a regular visitor to their home, and she was merely making an assumption that Peter was courting Caroline. Knowing how much you hate gossip, I made no inquiries."

Darcy returned to the window. "Blast it! Where is Bingley?" As soon as the phrase was uttered, a hackney pulled up in front of the house disgorging Charles, and after hurriedly paying the fare, he practically ran up the stairs. He had barely set one foot in the room before Darcy was demanding information. "Well?"

"It *is* true. Caroline and Peter Grayson are engaged," but by his looks, Charles understood that Darcy did not want him to say another word in front of Georgiana, who, understanding the exchange, quickly excused herself and was glad to do so. Not since the fiasco with George Wickham had she seen her brother so unsettled. Fortunately, this time, she was not the cause of his furrowed brow.

"Bingley, I need to know everything. This could greatly affect my sister, and I must know how this all came about."

"And I shall tell you all I know. But please keep in mind that I have very little control over what Caroline does. My father placed few restrictions on her inheritance, and she has ample reserves to do what she wants. And since she has informed me that she intends to move out of the house and in with our sister Diana until such time as she marries, she may come and go as she pleases. After all, she is twenty-two years old and not a child."

"I understand," Darcy answered, but he really didn't. Charles, as executor of his father's will, was in a position to assert great influence on his eight siblings, if necessary, by legal action. In Caroline's case, there would be the added benefit of reining in his sister's spending, a subject that was now common grist for the gossip mills. But Darcy knew that the amiable Bingley would do no such thing. "Please tell me what you have learned."

"Before speaking to Caroline, I first questioned Louisa, and she told me that after returning to town from Hertfordshire, Caroline threw herself into London's social life so that she might 'cleanse her mind of memories of you,' and it was at a private ball held in Portman Square where the couple first met.

"I then spoke to Caroline, who insisted it was Grayson who had sought an introduction, and knowing

4

that he was your cousin, she agreed. She said that the next day Grayson sent her a note saying how much he enjoyed her company, and so it began. Subsequent notes were accompanied by flowers and small gifts and carriage rides in St. James's Park. Grayson also made sure that she received invitations to those places where he would be in attendance. His intentions were obvious, and she was flattered by them. Three weeks later, he asked Caroline to become his wife, and she has accepted his offer.

"When you think about it, Darcy, why would she not accept such an offer? Grayson is extremely handsome, intelligent, and comes from a family with very high connections. I also understand he has a good income, and there are rumors circulating around town that he has plans for his estate in Derbyshire that will greatly increase its revenues."

Darcy was aware of Grayson's plans for his estate. By using Grayson Hall as collateral and trading on his expectations of inheriting Pemberley, Darcy's heir had approached several banking houses for loans. Because Pemberley had been mentioned, these same lenders had contacted Darcy. He had warned the bankers against advancing Grayson any monies as the improvements in question required his approval as they would also affect his property, and he was not inclined ato give it.

"Grayson has a very bright future," Charles added, glancing at his friend because it would be at the Darcys' expense that his wealth would grow.

"Did your sister say anything about me?" Darcy asked, saying nothing to Bingley about the loans. He had no wish to discuss family squabbles with his friend.

"Very little and all information was reluctantly given. However, she did acknowledge that Grayson had informed her that Pemberley was entailed away from the female line and that he was your heir. She was also aware that you and Grayson had quarreled. Caroline insists that the future disposition of the estate was not discussed, but I am not sure that I believe her because she appeared to be gloating over the fact that she was marrying the very person who, absent your having a son, will inherit Pemberley. When I suggested that a man who had such grand plans for his estate might need a wife with a large dowry, she became highly indignant and asked me to leave.

"Afterwards, I again spoke with Louisa, who said that Grayson has been every inch the gentleman, and that she, personally, has never heard Pemberley or the Darcys discussed at any time. And that, my friend, is all I have, except that the wedding will take place in three weeks' time at St. Margaret's. You are not invited."

Darcy poured a stiff brandy for himself and another for Bingley and settled into a chair, saying nothing. He could hardly take it all in. But one thing he did know was that he must act in order to protect Georgiana and Pemberley, and everything he did from this point onward must be directed toward that end.

"I have no words of comfort to offer you, my friend, and only a few words of advice," Charles said, reluctant to interrupt Darcy's thoughts, "and that is to state the obvious. You must marry and have a son. What else can you do?"

"Nothing. There is nothing else I can do. It is just that I had made plans to… Well, it does not matter what my plans were. I must quickly take a wife, and so I shall."

Chapter 2

Darcy summoned Jackson, his devoted butler, who also served as his social secretary when the Darcys were in town.

"Jackson, please bring me the guest list from last year's fête, and do we have a copy of that awful *The Insider*?"

"Yes, sir. It is very popular with the parlor maids."

"Of course, it is. How can one live without knowing what the Prince Regent or Lord Byron and his friends are doing? Thank you, Jackson."

While Darcy perused *The Insider*, Charles ran down the names of single ladies on the Darcy guest list.

"What about Letitia Montford?" Bingley asked.

"Have you ever had a conversation with her, Bingley? No, I didn't think so. Because if you had, you would not have suggested her. Nothing between the ears," and Darcy returned to the magazine. "Oh, bother! Susanna Hazelwood is engaged. Not my first choice, but she would have made the list."

"The younger daughter of the Earl of Henley is not married."

"Good grief, no! What if she is like Eleanor whose only purpose in life seems to be to torture my poor cousin, Lord Fitzwilliam."

"Oh, I forget they were married. Seeing how they are never together, it is easily forgotten. But what about Anne Tinsley? She is very nice."

"Yes, she is a lovely person, but would you want to wake up next to her?"

"Not the best looking girl, I will give you that. But then there is Claire Denton. I understand that she was the talk of the Taylors' ball."

"Yes, I heard that as well, but she is seventeen years old, a year younger than Georgiana, barely out of the nursery. But I shall put her on the list," which now had a grand total of one.

"Mrs. Conway?" Bingley said in a voice indicating his apprehension at its reception. "You like her very much. She is attractive, intelligent, politically connected, light on her feet, and has a pleasing figure."

Although it was never discussed, Bingley knew that Darcy and the widow of a prominent Whig politician had had an affair that lasted for more than a year. But to the surprise of many, the relationship had ended a few months earlier. The abrupt cessation of his visits had coincided with his sojourn at Netherfield Park, and there had been speculation that one of England's most sought-after bachelors had finally found a wife in the country. Such rumors had made it onto the pages of *The Insider* and may have been one of the reasons Caroline had thought Mr. Darcy was interested in her. But Bingley knew there was no one in the neighborhood of his leased estate who had caught his eye. Quite the contrary, he had been universally dismissive of his company stating at a local assembly that there was no one handsome enough to tempt him to dance, no less marry.

"I *do* like Mrs. Conway, but it is fairly certain that she cannot have children. Her husband had three sons by his first wife, but despite six years of marriage, Maria never conceived. Considering that the purpose of this exercise is to produce an heir, I cannot risk marrying where there is even a remote possibility that my wife is incapable of bearing children."

"Have you spoken to Georgiana? She has so many friends, and some of them are not as young as Miss Denton."

"No, nor shall I. She does not know that Peter and I have had a falling out, and if she did find out, she would be smart enough to realize that this could adversely affect her future." Darcy started to pace, and he was at risk of wearing out the carpet before he finally spoke. "Bingley, it is my fondest wish to find that I am in error and that I am judging my cousin too harshly. Although *I* have fallen out of favor with Peter, there is no reason to think that he is unhappy with Georgiana, whom he has always treated with the greatest kindness and affection. It may be that I am overreacting.

"I think I need to clear my mind and that it would be best for me to return to the country. If you don't mind, I would like to go to Netherfield Park." Since Bingley voiced no objection, Darcy continued. "Georgiana will be leaving in the morning to visit friends in Hampshire, so there is no reason to remain here. If I stay in town, I will be deluged with invitations, and if I do not go to my club for two nights in a row, some friend will come by to inquire after my health. With all these damn noises from the traffic in the street, I find it difficult to think. Besides, my thoughts are always clearest when I am in the country, and Netherfield is much closer than Pemberley."

"I shall order the carriage," Bingley said, pleased to be able to offer his friend a respite from his troubles.

* * *

As soon as Georgiana was in the door, she went in search of her brother and found him in his study reading, of all things, *The Insider*, a gossip rag that he absolutely despised. But she made no comment as she had more important things to discuss.

"I have just come from Augusta Selridge's house," Georgiana announced, omitting all niceties about how his day was progressing and the weather.

After rolling up the magazine in a failed attempt to hide the name of the magazine, Darcy responded with surprise. "I thought you considered Miss Selridge to be a gossip of the meanest sort and would have nothing to do with her?"

"I do and she is. But if one wants to find out what is going on in town that is where one must go."

"What did you learn from Miss Selridge?"

After removing her pelisse, bonnet, and gloves, and taking a seat near her brother as if to involve him in a conspiracy, Georgiana began. "It *is* true that Caroline Bingley is to marry our cousin on the fourteenth. Augusta knew this because Caroline had been there the previous day to share the good news with her. During her visit, Caroline declared that she is deeply in love with her betrothed and that she is looking forward to being the mistress of Grayson Hall. In speaking of the Grayson estate, she mentioned that the property abuts the Darcy estate and that it is very likely that she will one day be the Mistress of Pemberley as well because it is not likely that you will take a wife, the reason being that you prefer the company of a certain widow who provides you with all the benefits of marriage without any of the responsibilities."

An embarrassed Darcy looked away from his sister. She was only eighteen years old. What did she know about such things? She would imagine that he had sought Maria's company for the purpose of satisfying his physical needs. That was part of it, but certainly not all, as there were many women who would have been happy to oblige him in that regard. No, what he found so appealing about Mrs. Conway was her intelligent conversation and her understanding of a world that was growing more complicated by the day. There was a meeting of the minds whenever he was in her company.

"Do not trouble yourself about Mrs. Conway," Georgiana said in a sympathetic voice. "I already knew about her. I have been reading about you two in *The Insider* for the past year. And I know how you hate that magazine, but you did not specifically say I should not read it. You merely stated that it was written for small minds. I took your admonition as a suggestion."

Darcy merely smiled and unrolled the magazine to show his sister that he had been reading "the rag" himself.

"Thank you for not scolding me for engaging in gossip," Georgiana said after they had stopped laughing at the unveiling of *The Insider*. "But I have more to say about Peter, so I shall not ask why you are reading something that 'is not worth the paper it is printed on,' to quote an intelligent man. Although I was not completely sure, I suspected that you and he had quarreled because a few weeks ago, I encountered Peter in Rotten Row, and although he was very pleasant to me, he did not ask about you. Very odd I thought, and then I remembered that you and he had disagreed about some property north of Pemberley, and I thought that was possibly the reason for his not sending his regards. Did I guess correctly?"

"Yes, you did. And since you have worked your way through so much of this puzzle, I shall tell you that with Peter's engagement to Caroline Bingley, I have grave concerns that if I should die that you will be asked to leave Pemberley. Since he has no claim on this house, as it came to us through our mother, you will never be without a home of your own. However, you will be deprived of all income generated by the estate. We certainly have other resources, but Pemberley remains the single greatest source of our wealth."

Georgiana looked puzzled. "Forgive me if my questions appear intrusive, but as mean-spirited as Caroline is, there is nothing to say that Peter might not marry someone who is equally unpleasant or even worse than she is. Because I am your sister and Caroline believes that she was treated unfairly by you, I know that she would enjoy showing me the door, but there are scores of women who would do the same without giving it a second thought. What has changed?"

"Georgiana, there are things you do not know. Everything is not always as it seems."

"Can you give me an example?"

How did Darcy tell his sister that he had paid little attention to Peter's possible choice of a wife because he had believed that there would never be a wife? Peter's inclinations were such that Darcy believed he would have a greater interest in Charles than Caroline. With the exception of Beau Brummel, he knew of no other man with such a passion for fine clothes and other frippery, and the amount of time his cousin spent preparing for an evening on the town equaled that of a duchess making an appearance at court. To the best of Darcy's knowledge, Peter had shown no interest in any woman and rarely attended dances and other entertainments where he would meet ladies who were his equal in society. Because of these observations, he had imagined that his cousin would remain a bachelor, and if he inherited Pemberley, Georgiana would be asked to stay on to supervise the running of the household.

"I confess that I do not understand what you are trying *not* to tell me, but the heart of the matter is that you do not want Peter and Caroline to inherit Pemberley. In order to achieve the desired end, you must find a wife and father a son as quickly as possible." Georgiana responded to her brother's surprised look by telling him that she had seen the guest list for last season's fête. "I found it in the parlor, and I was puzzled as to why it was there because I knew exactly where I had placed it. So I surmised that you must have asked Mr. Jackson to bring it to you. I was going over it when I saw these tiny dots next to some of the ladies' names, all of whom were unmarried, and putting two and two together, I came up with one sister-in-law."

"You seem to have a knack for taking unrelated bits of information and weaving them into a cohesive whole. Have you considered becoming a reporter for *The Insider* where you would not be burdened by things so irrelevant as facts?"

"I would love to become a reporter, but I have more important work to do here." She took his hand in hers. "Will, I remember so little of our mother. But what I do recall is that she was deeply in love with Papa, and when you marry, I want you to be profoundly in love with your wife. So you must put away that list as there is no one on it who is worthy of you, and you must look elsewhere."

"Georgie, you are all grown up. When did this happen?"

"Last year, and it happened because of that unfortunate episode with Wickham. It is hard to remain a little girl when you have seen such wickedness. But I have no wish to speak of that scoundrel, but of you. So you must promise me that you will not settle and that you will marry for love."

"I shall do my very best. Is there anything else?"

"Yes, you must take care of your health. I will gladly yield the title of Mistress of Pemberley to the woman you love, but I will not give it up to Caroline Bingley without a fight."

Chapter 3

When Elizabeth arrived at Netherfield, she was relieved to learn from her sister that the big decision regarding the draperies for the dining room had been made: blue with a gold embossed diamond pattern. If only such a favorable outcome had been achieved with regard to the draperies in the drawing room, Lizzy would have felt safe in visiting her sister more often. Knowing that the interiors of Netherfield were outdated, she had expected that Jane would want to make a few changes, but she had no idea that it would become Jane's life's work, and by extension, her own.

"I have had another letter from Charles," Jane said. "He will leave London on Wednesday. I am eagerly looking forward to his return."

"So am I," Lizzy said, pointing her chin in the direction of the windows. She would be happy to relinquish her role as design advisor and pass on the fabric swatches to her brother-in-law.

"He comes with Mr. Darcy," Jane shot back.

"I take that back," Lizzy said, laughing. "Your husband may stay in town for as long as he likes so that Mr. Darcy might remain there as well."

"Lizzy, why do you dislike Mr. Darcy so much? It is not like you to dwell on a slight."

"It is not I who dislikes Mr. Darcy. It is Mr. Darcy who dislikes me. And it is not just a matter of his saying that I was merely tolerable but not handsome enough to tempt him to dance. He also accused me of willfully misunderstanding people."

"But only after you accused him of implacable resentment and of hating everybody."

"Yes, that *was* a rather harsh statement that I no longer believe. He does not hate everybody; he merely *dislikes* a lot of people."

"Well, I hope you will be kind to Mr. Darcy as his troubles mount in London."

Lizzy was aware that Mr. Darcy was unhappy with the announced engagement of Caroline Bingley to his cousin, Peter Grayson. She had not known that the Pemberley estate and Longbourn shared a similar fate: They were both entailed away from the female line.

"It is still a bit of a muddle to me," Jane said. "Writing letters is not Charles's strong suit. He writes so fast that he has a tendency to drop words. A lot of times it is the word 'not' that is omitted, making his sentences contradictory. But my understanding is that Mr. Grayson and Mr. Darcy recently quarreled over the building of manufactories on their adjacent properties in Derbyshire. Apparently, Mr. Darcy finds it curious that such a young man, Mr. Grayson is only three and twenty, should wish to marry and that he has chosen Caroline Bingley, someone whom he did not know a month ago. He is asking himself 'why Caroline?' It seems that Mr. Darcy has decided that he must protect his sister and Pemberley from his cousin, and after a brief visit here at Netherfield, he will return to London for the purpose of finding a wife."

"Well, that should not be too difficult. If you read *The Insider*, you will see that his name is connected to virtually every unattached girl, woman, or widow in high society. He must have an awful lot of energy to wait on so many ladies."

"Charles says it is all nonsense. If Mr. Darcy so much as walks into the room where there is a lady in need of a husband, the next day both of their names appear in the gossip sheets as if they had fallen into each other's arms."

"Well, it is understandable why the ladies act in such a way. He *is* handsome, rich, intelligent, and, most importantly, eligible."

"Lizzy, those are the first nice things I have ever heard you say about Mr. Darcy."

"I am merely stating the facts, Jane. My opinion of Mr. Darcy remains unchanged."

* * *

"Bingley, I greatly appreciate this," Darcy said as the carriage rolled down the road toward Hertfordshire. "After all, you have been married for little more than three months, and yet you agreed to leave your lovely bride to come to the aid of a friend."

"Knowing of our long friendship, Jane completely understands. Besides, I have an interest in this matter as well. Even before this engagement business, I had planned to go to town because I had written two letters to Caroline and another to Louisa, neither of whom responded. Very suspicious, especially on Louisa's part as she is always prompt in replying to my letters. Apparently, Caroline swore her to silence about her friendship with Grayson.

"And just because I am married, you need not make yourself scarce," Bingley continued. "After all, Jane and I spent three lovely weeks at your villa in Weymouth. I understand that your intention was to provide your newly-married friend with some time to be alone with his bride, but Jane is already encouraging me to find other ways of entertaining myself. I am willing to do so as my wife has a new project that I have absolutely no interest in. As we speak, my wife is knee deep in fabric. As soon as she received permission from the Darlingtons to change the draperies in the dining and drawing rooms, she made it her top priority. I had no idea she hated those drapes so much."

"How different she is from her sister, Elizabeth," Darcy said. "I cannot imagine her investing so much time in choosing fabric."

"That is so true. Whenever Elizabeth came to Netherfield, I could hear the pair of them talking about Jane's redecorating schemes. It usually consisted of Jane begging her sister to pay attention to the matter at hand, but with little success. But they seem to delight in their differences and in each other's company."

"I did notice that whenever I visited, Elizabeth absented herself from Netherfield Park. I am afraid that she has never forgiven me for that testy exchange we had about pride versus vanity."

"Oh, no! That is not why she does not come. She thinks you do not like *her*," Bingley said. "She told me so herself, and she fears that her presence would result in an unpleasant visit. I told her that she was wrong, but it made no difference. I am sure these things will be sorted out over time, that is, if you keep your strong opinions to yourself."

Darcy laughed. Yes, he did have strong opinions, but they were mild when compared to Elizabeth Bennet's. With the exception of Mrs. Conway, who was a dozen years older than Elizabeth and who was used to heated political debate, he knew of no other lady who refused to temper her speech to suit her audience. Facts were facts, and they should not be shied away from. If you asked her a question, by Jove, you had better be prepared to hear the answer. Although he had been on the receiving end of some of her strong opinions, he respected her honesty, and there was no other virtue he admired more.

* * *

To celebrate Mr. Bingley's return to Netherfield Park, Jane invited all of the Bennets to supper. Even though Mrs. Bennet had been in the manor house a dozen times, whenever she visited, she was positively giddy at the thought that her Jane had married someone who had enough money to afford the lease on such an estate. She was especially pleased when her daughter showed her the fabric she had chosen for the dining room draperies because that meant that Charles and Jane would remain at Netherfield for at least awhile longer and that would allow her to mention the couple at every possible opportunity whilst in Meryton or visiting with her neighbors, especially Lady Lucas. Unfortunately, her excitement in dining in such elegant surroundings brought out the worst in her: she talked too much and too loudly and was guilty of speaking of matters that were best left unspoken, especially when it came to the anticipated arrival of little Bingleys.

Lydia and Kitty were even sillier than their mother. They had little to say that did not involve the officers who were serving in a regiment of militia encamped near Meryton. Mary's pontifications had past the point of being merely tedious to downright annoying, and she was aided in this by her correspondence with her cousin, the Reverend William Collins, with whom she was exchanging lengthy dissertations on subjects of no interest to anyone other than themselves.

And while Mr. Darcy watched the Bennets, Elizabeth watched Mr. Darcy. Although he said little, his face showed a great deal, and from his expressions Lizzy knew that his low opinion of her family was being confirmed with every syllable uttered by her mother and sisters. But she could not blame him. Her family behaved badly and that was a fact.

Chapter 4

As Darcy lay in bed, the rain pummeled the manor house and the tree branches bowed and scraped against the windows. There was nothing that provided a more appropriate backdrop for his thoughts than this act of nature. It also provided clarity. He suspected that the reason he had chosen to return to Hertfordshire was because the answer to his difficulties was here. From the moment he had learned of Caroline Bingley's engagement to Peter Grayson, he had been moving in one direction and that the list of prospective brides had been for show because he already knew whom he would ask to be his wife.

Darcy rose from the chair and took out a piece of stationery and began the letter he had been composing in his head for more than a week now. He had made his decision, and now it was time to act on it.

* * *

"Lizzy, I was coming to look for you. Come into my room," Mr. Bennet said, his distress evident in his voice and demeanor. Elizabeth followed him into his study and determined that the cause of his unhappiness was the paper he held in his hand.

"I have received a letter this morning that has astonished me exceedingly. But I shall not keep you in suspense as to its contênts," and he handed a sealed letter to his daughter. Looking at the seal, Lizzy was puzzled. How could her father possibly know what was in the unopened letter, and understanding her confusion, Mr. Bennet explained that the writer had first requested permission to be allowed to write to his daughter and had summarized its contents.

Why all the mystery, Lizzy wondered? Why could Papa not just say who it was from and what it was about? It was all so puzzling, and even more so after she had finished reading and rereading the letter. Lizzy thought that there must be some mistake, but no, there was his signature. It was real. But it did not make any sense.

"I don't understand." Lizzy said.

"Read it again, girl. It is all there, plain as day. Mr. Darcy wants to marry you."

"But I just saw him the other evening, and he barely uttered two sentences to me."

"I cannot even pretend to understand his motives for choosing you of all people, to be his wife, but you must take pen in hand and respond immediately. Thank him for the honor of his proposal but tell him that it is impossible for you to accept him."

While staring at the letter, Lizzy quickly ran through her mind every time the two of them had been together. Meryton had been a disaster as he had been rude in the extreme when he had commented that he was "in no humor to give consequence to young ladies who are slighted by other men." Her reaction had been to respond in kind by snubbing him at Lucas Lodge. But she had to admit that during her stay at Netherfield Park whilst she had been nursing Jane that there had been a softening in his looks when he glanced at her, and she had detected some admiration on his part for her willingness to stand up to the barbs and left-handed compliments of Mr. Bingley's sisters.

In the weeks leading up to the wedding, she had seen little of him, but when she had been in his company, he had been all politeness. But other than the occasional guarded look, he had paid her no particular notice. At Jane and Charles's wedding, their conversation had been little more than an exercise in civil discourse demanded by the occasion, and even those exchanges would not have taken place if he had not been Charles's closest friend and she the sister of the bride. In conclusion, she had no idea what Mr. Darcy thought about her, except, apparently, that he wanted to marry her. How very odd.

"Lizzy, why do you hesitate?" her father asked in response to her silence. "This man, who never looked at you without seeing a blemish, wishes to make you his wife." Lizzy, still stunned by the revelation enclosed in the letter, said nothing, and her father could see that she was actually thinking about accepting him. "Are you out of your senses to be considering this proposal? Have you not always hated him?"

"No, Papa, I do not hate him. Although his behavior in Hertfordshire was less than stellar, he *is* a man or honor and dignity, and my opinion of him has recently altered. I did not give him enough credit for being the friend of Mr. Bingley, a man whose station in life is decidedly beneath his own, and when he speaks of his sister, he is a different man altogether. I cannot believe that someone who cares so much about his family and friends can be devoid of all goodness."

"Do not think that I am ignorant of the real reason why you are entertaining this offer," her agitated father responded. "This is about the entail. But I will not allow you to sacrifice yourself on that account. There are other possibilities. Perhaps, we may convince Mr. Collins to marry Mary."

"Papa, this involves a lot more than the entail."

"Well, then let me advise you to think better of this proposal. To be sure, he is rich and you will have fine clothes and carriages, but he cannot make you happy. I know you, and I know that unless you truly esteem your husband that happiness will elude you."

"I am not saying that I shall accept Mr. Darcy's offer, and since you have read a summary of his letter, you know that he is not assuming that I shall say 'yes.' But his offer does merit careful consideration. You and I both know that my chances of receiving *any* offer of marriage are not good. There is not a man in this neighborhood who could afford to take a wife with such a meager fortune, and despite Aunt Gardiner's best efforts, no one in London showed more than a passing interest in me because of my lack of a dowry. All I am saying is that it is an offer worthy of my attention."

Mr. Bennet continued to shake his head. "This is all my fault. If I had taken better care of my family, we would not be in such dire straits." Lizzy gestured for her father to join her by the fire. "Dear Papa, you could not have known that you would have five daughters and no sons. Under the circumstances, you have done your best, and there is no need for recrimination."

"Lizzy, let me not have the grief of seeing you unable to respect your partner in life," he said, as they listened to Mrs. Bennet in a nearby room giggling with Lydia.

"I can spare you that grief, Papa, because I *do* respect Mr. Darcy. I may not like him all that much, but he *is* a man of worthy of my respect."

Chapter 5

Jane made her way across the pastureland and down the lane connecting Netherfield Park to Longbourn, winding her way through grass wet with dew to a giant weeping willow tree that had once served as a hiding place for a youthful Jane and Lizzy. Despite it being a windy and damp day, Jane's curiosity as to the reason Lizzy had asked to meet her at their secret place drove her onward.

As soon as Lizzy saw Jane, she ran toward her and gave her a huge hug, which immediately raised the alarm for Jane. Lizzy was affectionate, but not particularly demonstrative. Something was definitely wrong.

"Thank you for coming on such short notice. I assume you followed my instructions and did not tell Charles you were coming to meet me."

"There was no need to say anything to Charles as he has gone riding with Mr. Darcy and said that he would be out all morning. Lizzy, what is this about?"

"This letter explains all," and Lizzy handed Jane Mr. Darcy's letter.

Dear Miss Elizabeth,

I hope you will forgive the liberty I am taking in writing to you without first receiving permission to do so, but a matter of great concern to my family has caused me to act.

I understand from Charles that you are aware that Caroline Bingley has recently become engaged to my cousin, Peter Grayson, who also happens to be the heir to Pemberley as the estate is entailed away from the female line, and my sister cannot inherit. I have reason to suspect that there are ulterior motives for his choosing to marry at this time.

Because of this turn of events, I realize that my plans to wed only after my sister had found a husband must be put aside and that I must take a wife and have a son. This is the reason for this letter. I am most humbly making an offer of marriage to you. If you consent to be my wife, I would hope that we might marry as soon as possible. Because this is an event of great importance, I am sure you will have many, many questions to ask of me, and I will answer all of them to the best of my ability. Please be assured that you will receive a generous marriage settlement as well as a yearly allowance sufficient to meet all your personal needs.

If this is a matter you wish to pursue, please let me know where and when you wish to discuss it. Yours, Fitzwilliam Darcy

Like Lot's wife, Jane stood frozen in place, starring at the letter, and although her mouth was open, no words came out.

"Jane, please say something."

"This is the most remarkable thing I have ever read in my life. If I did not recognize Mr. Darcy's handwriting, I would say that it was a prank."

"This is no prank, Jane. Mr. Darcy is in earnest."

"Are you thinking about accepting him?" Considering their history, Jane could hardly believe it.

"I *have* to consider it. You know my prospects: I have none. Since Charles and you married, Charlotte and I speak of little else as the specter of spinsterhood looms before us. And let me remind you what Aunt Susan said last Christmas: 'Elizabeth, you will never marry. You favor your own opinions too much?' She was right. But Mr. Darcy knows that I am not inclined to withhold my opinion just because I am a female, which makes his offer all the more puzzling."

"But you do not love him, and it is unlikely that you ever will."

"Again, what choice do I have? If you think about it, there is much to be gained by marrying Mr. Darcy. I will be financially secure for the rest of my life as will our mother and sisters."

"But now that I am married to Mr. Bingley that is less of a concern," Jane said, trying desperately to give her sister a reason to decline Mr. Darcy's offer.

"Yes, that is true. Mr. Bingley is a very kind man, but is it right to expect him to carry the whole Bennet family on his back? And soon enough, he will have his own family to care for."

"Yes, very soon."

"Jane, are you…?"

"Not that I know of, but considering the frequency, it is likely that something will happen soon. And that is another thing. Lizzy, I cannot begin to describe how intimate the marriage act is."

"Well, you do not have to. I am not devoid of an imagination, and we did grow up on a farm."

"It can be a wonderful experience, if you are in love, but you are not."

"I am well aware of that, Jane. And since the reason for the marriage is to produce a son, I have no illusions as to this being a romantic liaison. But you should not worry. I have not positively decided in favor of accepting his offer. First, I must ask him: 'Why have you chosen to make me an offer and not someone whose situation in life is closer to your own?'"

"So you must first have a meeting. When will that be?"

"As soon as he answers this letter," and Lizzy handed Jane her response.

Chapter 6

While Darcy waited for Elizabeth to arrive at Netherfield, he reread the note in which she had agreed at least to consider his proposal. In light of their contentious history, he had been greatly relieved that he not been rejected out of hand, and as the minutes went by, he mentally prepared for the meeting in much the same way as a barrister would who was coming before the bar to argue his case.

During their meeting near the willow tree, Jane had offered to prepare a light meal before the negotiations got under way, but Lizzy had declined. When she was anxious, she had no appetite, and her level of anxiety was as high as it had ever been. When she arrived at Netherfield, she was told that Mr. Darcy was waiting for her in the parlor, and after squeezing her sister's hand and taking a deep breath, Lizzy opened the double doors. Before her stood the man who might very well become her husband. He was elegantly dressed, and the fact that he had chosen to wear his finest clothes indicated that he wished to make a good impression, and she was touched by the care he had taken on her behalf.

"Thank you for agreeing to come to Netherfield," Darcy said.

After pleasantries were exchanged, Lizzy got to the heart of the matter. "Please allow me to thank you for honoring me with an offer of marriage. However, there are so many questions in need of answers."

"I understand, and as indicated in my letter, I am prepared to answer each question to your satisfaction. But, perhaps, if I provide some background information as to the necessity of my making such an unexpected offer, many of your questions will be answered."

With his facts at the ready, Darcy explained that his grandfather, Edward Darcy, had been married three times. "His first wife was my father's mother, a fine woman, whom he dearly loved. However, according to my grandfather, he had subsequently married 'two fools,' who, between them, had provided him with 'three silly daughters.' By the time his third wife had died, Edward Darcy, a difficult man on his best day, held a very low opinion of females, which is why he placed the entail on the estate for two generations, and although it will end with the next generation, that provision does not help me or Georgiana."

"And you have concerns about how your heir, Peter Grayson, will treat your sister?"

"Yes, and allow me to explain. Peter was orphaned at the age of sixteen, and my father served as his guardian for three years. When my father died, his guardianship passed to me for an additional two years. Although it was an infrequent event, my father and I occasionally denied Peter's request for money, and it seems that he resented our interference. I did not know this until I went to speak to him about his engagement to Miss Bingley.

"What I *did* know was that Peter, who is only three and twenty and given to occasional fits of pique, was upset with me with regard to another matter. Because the income from his estate does not provide sufficient monies to meet his needs, he devised a scheme to build several manufactories near a stream that runs through our two estates. I opposed his plan because it would pollute the water that irrigates Pemberley's gardens. Since he could not go forward without my cooperation, we quarreled."

"But how did he come to know Caroline Bingley?"

"Exactly! How *did* he come to know her? I could hardly believe that it was a coincidence, and I was right." Darcy stood up and started to pace. Lizzy could see that he was agitated, which was his normal state whenever Caroline was involved. "I am sure from Caroline's marked attentions to me at Netherfield that you are aware that she wished for me to make her an offer of marriage," and Lizzy nodded, "but I never considered it. In fact, she was such a source of annoyance to me that I would return to town just to be free of her company. I should have remained in London, but Bingley would write to me, pleading with me to return, and so I did. And in doing so, I gave Caroline the impression that it was she who was drawing me back to Hertfordshire. When she finally realized that no offer would be made, she was very angry with me.

"Feeling ill used, when Caroline returned to town, she told anyone who would listen that I had played lightly with her affections and that I had behaved in an ungentlemanlike manner. With the gossip mill fully engaged, word of this reached Peter, who sought her out. He told me that his purpose was to commiserate with someone who had also been badly treated by me. But, instead of merely finding a sympathetic ear, he tells me that he fell in love with her. I only hope that it is true and that it is not her £20,000 that he loves.

"But do you see my problem? If I should be taken by a sudden illness or killed in an accident before marrying and producing a male heir, it is Caroline and Peter who will reside at Pemberley. Can you imagine the treatment Georgiana would receive from two people who felt that they had suffered at her brother's hand? I simply cannot risk it."

It was now clear to Lizzy why Mr. Darcy was in need of a wife—and quickly, but it still didn't answer her main question.

"Mr. Darcy, I sympathize with your predicament, and I understand the reasons why you must marry. But why me? In truth, you know no good of me, and you have earlier withstood my beauty."

"Of course, you are referring to that unfortunate comment I made within your hearing at the Netherfield ball. I was not only rude, but wrong. It is many months since I have considered you to be one of the handsomest women of my acquaintance."

This statement took Lizzy by surprise. Mr. Darcy thought she was one of the prettiest ladies he knew? *Well, that is quite a compliment considering the company he must keep in London.*

"Miss Elizabeth, I can assure you that you have much to recommend you other than a pretty face."

"Is it my impertinence you admire?" she asked, but then shook her head indicating that that could not possibly be the case. "You know me to be a person who speaks her mind, and I know there were times when you took great offense because I was so vocal in stating my opinions. Despite evidence of my propensity to speak what I find, you are still asking me to be your wife. If you think that I shall change, Mr. Darcy, you are quite wrong. My frankness is so much a part of my nature that I believe that I am incapable of alteration."

Lizzy waited for some sign that Mr. Darcy now realized how ill suited she was by temperament to be his wife. After he gave no indication that anything she said had changed his mind, she concluded by saying, "Surely, there are women in London society who could provide you with a son who are your equal in rank."

"Lest you think that I have not given careful consideration to this matter, let me assure you that I have thought of little else since I learned of the engagement. I will confess that I am greatly unsettled by this business with Peter. There were other schemes that I could have supported that would have provided him with an income, but, instead, he made promises to venturers and approached bankers without first consulting me. And this business with Caroline. To think that he deliberately sought out someone because he thought she disliked me even more than he did. It leaves a bad taste in my mouth.

"As for London society, yes, it is true that there are many unattached ladies who are superior to you in rank, but I also find that many are conceited and selfish and place a greater value on fashion and the outward appearances of wealth and rank than on character. So, ironically, it is because of your honest remarks that I have asked you to be my wife, and although I have been on the receiving end of your frank assessments, I know that they are honestly made and without malice. I cannot say the same for the ladies of London society. In brief, I can trust you."

There were more matters to be discussed: opposition to the union by friends and family, his expectations for the marriage, the marriage settlement and her yearly allowance, management of Pemberley, and many more, but even after everything was explained in detail, Lizzy hesitated. The cold hard fact was that Mr. Darcy did not love her. The marriage would be similar to those arranged among heads of state and members of the nobility and for the same reason: to produce a male heir. Could she do it?

"I thank you for answering all of my questions, but I am still not ready to accept your offer. Before making a decision, there are two things that I ask. The first is that I should meet Miss Darcy. It is obvious that you care deeply for your sister, and since she will be greatly affected by my decision, I would like to visit with her. Secondly, I wish to see Pemberley. I am not convinced that I am capable of managing such a great estate, and I have no wish to disappoint you."

Darcy readily agreed to both conditions and was pleased that she had thought it important to meet Georgiana before deciding. She had put the interests of his sister before her own, and in doing so, had provided further evidence that he had chosen well.

Chapter 7

Georgiana could not stop looking at her brother. With her eyes wide and her mouth agape, she listened to the details of Will's offer of marriage to Elizabeth Bennet of Longbourn, Hertfordshire, a lady completely unknown to her. In fact, up until a half hour ago, she had never heard the lady's name mentioned, not even in casual conversation.

"What is her middle name?" Georgiana asked when Darcy had finally finished revealing all of the details of his proposal.

"I do not know. I am not sure that she even has one? Why? Is that important?"

"Of course, it is important. It is my intention to embroider her initials on a pillow. Perhaps, she was named after her mother. That is a common practice. What is Mrs. Bennet's Christian name?"

"I have no idea. I do know that Mr. Bennet's first name is Thomas."

"Well, that is not particularly helpful."

Darcy could see the wheels spinning in his sister's head. She was planning a great wedding and breakfast where these things might actually matter, and she would be disappointed when she learned that Elizabeth and he would stand where their parents had stood, in St. Michael's church, Lambton, with few in attendance.

"You know I have suspected all along that you had taken a fancy to a Hertfordshire lass."

"I see that you have been spending some time with Robbie Burns."

Darcy found his sister's adoption of the patois of the characters in her books and poems to be adorable, and it was a source of laughter for both of them. But not today. She would not be diverted.

"The reason I thought someone might have touched your heart is because whenever you returned from visiting Mr. Bingley you always looked out of sorts. Is not discomposure evidence that one has fallen in love?"

"Georgiana, this is not the plot from one of your novels."

"I know that, and even though you do not approve of my choice of fiction, these books are popular because they speak to our greatest passions. They document those sentiments that have echoed throughout the ages. Is there anything new since Orpheus loved Eurydice?"

"Yes, stories with happy endings," her brother said, smiling.

"Will, please tell me all you know about Miss Elizabeth," Georgiana asked, ignoring her brother's comment.

Although Darcy had been almost legalistic in listing the details of his offer, he had said very little about the lady, an omission that Georgiana insisted he correct.

"It is my understanding that the education of the two eldest Bennet daughters was undertaken by their grandmother, the wife of a solicitor, and that Elizabeth does speak passable French. And although she does not play the pianoforte as well as you do, she plays a lively tune, and she has a fine singing voice."

"Are you planning to marry the lady or to exhibit her?" Georgiana asked with a frown. This was not what she wanted to hear. "What does she look like?"

"Well, she is about two inches shorter than you are, so let us say 5'-2". She has a pleasing figure and a well-turned ankle. Her face is not symmetrical, but, still, she is quite pleasant to look at. She has curly, dark brown hair. But it is her eyes that are her best feature. They sparkle and have a hint of mischief in them. She often looks as if she is making plans to dump a bucket of water over someone's head."

"Like you did to our cousin, Colonel Fitzwilliam?" Georgiana asked, laughing.

"Exactly. But with Elizabeth, I would know when she was up to such mischief because her eyes reveal all. When she was angry with me, I knew it."

"Elizabeth was angry with you?" Furrows appeared in Georgiana's brow.

Fearing that he had opened a can of worms and that his sister would pepper him with questions about the cause of the lady's anger, he sought to reassure her. "It was when we first met, shortly after my arrival in Hertfordshire. Bingley insisted that I attend a local assembly. I was in no humor to do so, and so I…"

"…behaved badly. I know exactly how you are when you are in ill humor."

"In my defense, was it absolutely necessary for us to attend an assembly two days after my arrival?"

"How inconsiderate of Mr. Bingley. The date of the assembly should have been changed to a time more convenient to you." She gave him an impish smile.

"You are supposed to be *defending* your brother, not taking him to task. Where is your loyalty?" Darcy asked in a teasing voice. He delighted in this type of exchange, especially since Georgiana had repeatedly demonstrated that she understood the difference between private and public discourse and that she knew when he was serious and when he had had enough of her teasing. "So now to bed as you have exhausted me with all your probing questions." But he was quite sure that the inquisition would continue in the morning.

* * *

The next morning, Georgiana came to the breakfast room with a head full of ideas. Her first suggestion to her brother was that Elizabeth and she go to Pemberley without him, thus providing the two ladies with an opportunity to visit and to get to know each other without Darcy watching for clues as to how the pair was getting along.

"While Elizabeth and I are at Pemberley visiting, I suggest that you go to Derby and stay with the Hulstons," Georgiana said. "From your description of the lady, I anticipate that we shall get along famously, and once she sees how the servants actually run Pemberley, her fears on that account will be put to rest. I shall then write to you at Hulston Hall, and you may come to Pemberley and visit with the vicar and make arrangements for the wedding. Is that agreeable?"

Darcy mulled over the plan, and in doing so, he could not find any fault with it. *If* everything did go as well as Georgiana hoped it would, then Elizabeth and he could go to St. Michael's to arrange for the banns to be announced. After that, he would return to Hertfordshire and formally request Elizabeth's hand in marriage from Mr. Bennet.

"Yes, it is a good plan, and if all goes well, we shall be married within the month."

"Oh, Will, I am very glad that you have found someone to love."

"Georgie, I did not say that I loved Miss Elizabeth. For the present it is enough that I like her very much."

Chapter 8

Georgiana and Elizabeth departed for Derbyshire from
Netherfield Park, and with the lengthy carriage ride
before them, Lizzy was wondering what they would say
to each other during their many hours together. But she
need not have worried. As soon as Mrs. Brotherton,
Georgiana's companion, dozed off, the young lady was
off and running.

"I am so pleased that we shall have an opportunity
to get to know each other without Will being present. I
do not think he realizes how formidable he appears
when he stops, stares, and says little."

*So this is not behavior reserved just for strangers,
but intimates suffer under his gaze as well* is what Lizzy
thought, but what she said out loud was: "I do think
that because of his taciturn nature there are those who
find him to be somewhat intimidating. But I have found
that on further acquaintance, he does soften—a bit."

"Oh, I can assure you that when he is completely
comfortable with his company he is funny and engaging
and quite charming."

Those were not words that Lizzy would have used to describe Mr. Darcy, but who knew him better than his sister? And could the amiable Charles Bingley really be a friend to someone who was always dour? The conversation then turned to Miss Darcy's companion, who had been with Georgiana for a little more than a year.

"She is very different from my former companion, Mrs. Younge, as she is a much more maternal figure and exactly what I need. Her advice is excellent, and since I shall be coming out in the spring, Mrs. Brotherton says that I must always act as if people are watching me. In that way, I shall always be at my best." After lifting her hands that were neatly folded on her lap and pointing to her crossed ankles, she added, "You see that I follow her advice."

"I agree that that is excellent advice when you are in a public forum. But you are with a friend, and my legs are not crossed," Lizzy said, lifting her feet and wiggling them. "It is too long a ride to hold such a pose," and Georgiana happily uncrossed her ankles.

With little prompting, Lizzy's young friend shared everything she knew of the Darcy family history, including touching stories about her beloved father and the few memories she had of her mother, who had died when she was only eight. But her most endearing stories were reserved for Mr. Darcy, who was brother, father, guardian, and friend to her. The picture she painted bore little resemblance to the Fitzwilliam Darcy whom Lizzy had met at the Meryton assembly, and if Georgiana's role had been to convince Lizzy to marry her brother, then she was doing an admirable job of it.

* * *

"I hope you like dogs," Georgiana said, as they approached Hulston Hall on the second day of their journey. "Sir Edward has four children, and each is allowed to have his or her own pet. Every dog is of a different breed, and since there are male and females, well, there are also puppies. The pairings have resulted in some very funny looking creatures."

"I *do* like dogs, but since the death of my mother's little terrier, all of our dogs are ones that work on the farm and earn their keep."

Georgiana, who had decided to leave her little pugs, Salt and Pepper, behind in London, assured Elizabeth that she could have any breed of dog she liked. However, she warned her that they must get along with Darcy's whippets, David and Goliath. "They have the run of the manor house and are hopelessly spoiled by my brother. The hardest thing you may have to do at Pemberley is to get those two dogs to like you."

The carriage was met in the courtyard of Hulston Hall by a hodgepodge of barking and baying canines that were jumping up and down in an attempt to see who was in the conveyance. The house, badly in need of repair, had been built during the Jacobean Era. Lacking in any rational plan, it was a red-brick box with two towers slapped onto either end of it and with a series of additions protruding from its rear, but when Lizzy met Sir Edward and his family, the haphazardly-built house seemed to fit them perfectly.

During her brief stay, Lizzy learned of yet another side to Mr. Darcy: the hunter, the equestrian, the man who came to this remote setting to shoot and to fish, and from Sir Edward's stories, a man who enjoyed teasing his friend of many years and who was teased by him in his turn. This was the Mr. Darcy that Charles Bingley knew, and Lizzy now had a better understanding of their friendship.

But tomorrow the travelers would arrive at Pemberley where she would have to decide if she could or if she wanted to be the mistress of such a great estate, and she thought of Longbourn and the warmth of its small rooms and the closeness of her family. Could she replicate that environment in a great country manor house with a man who had married her only because he needed an heir? Tomorrow would tell.

Chapter 9

As the carriage entered the long drive to Pemberley, Georgiana informed her new friend that she would leave most of the telling of the history of the house to Mrs. Reynolds, and if there was anything she wanted to know about the manor after speaking with the housekeeper, an unlikely outcome, she could ask Mr. Jackson, the Darcy butler, when he returned from town. "*Or* you could ask Will when he arrives as he has a great interest in history, not only of Pemberley, but the region as well, as we are very close to the Peak."

As she waited for the storied Pemberley to come into view, Lizzy could feel her heart pounding and her head pulsing. Because Caroline Bingley had once imagined that she would be the mistress of this great house, she had described the manor in glowing terms. Had Caroline exaggerated its charms, she wondered? No, she had not. As the carriage climbed a gentle rise, there stood before her a beautiful Georgian stone mansion, dominating the landscape, and glowing in the afternoon sun. It was so elegant in its simplicity and so perfectly situated that it nearly took Lizzy's breath away. *And of this I might be mistress*, she thought as the manor house filled her carriage window.

As soon as the conveyance came to a stop, footmen in livery appeared and quickly assisted the passengers before seeing to their baggage. Georgiana acknowledged their efforts with a nod, but Lizzy thought how different things were at Longbourn. The Bennets had always had servants, but they were so integrated into the fabric of the family that births were acknowledged with great fanfare, marriages joyfully celebrated, and deaths mourned. Lizzy wondered if Georgiana and her brother even knew the names of the junior servants who waited upon them.

Unsure of her decision regarding Mr. Darcy, Lizzy thought it best to keep the possibility of a marriage hidden from Mrs. Reynolds until she had made up her mind, and she had advised Georgiana to say nothing. As far as the housekeeper knew, she was a friend of Miss Darcy's, nothing more.

Lizzy stepped into the two-story foyer, which was dominated by an elaborate wrought-iron twin staircase. The interiors had been done in the manner of Robert Adam, a favorite of Jane's, and one whose decorative style would be employed when Bingley Manor was built. Lizzy loved it as well. Who could not—with its soft colors and elegant neoclassical touches?

Georgiana quickly spirited Elizabeth up the staircase to the suite of rooms that had once belonged to Lady Anne Darcy. If she became Mrs. Fitzwilliam Darcy, these rooms would become her own, and the first thing that Lizzy saw upon entering the sitting room was a portrait of Mr. Darcy's mother with her lightly-powdered hair, enormous hat, and the frilly frocks so favored by that generation. On her lap sat Georgiana, who was probably three years old, with her older brother standing next to her, and it brought tears to her eyes knowing that their mother had been taken from them just a few years after the painting had been completed. The resemblance between mother and daughter was striking: light brown hair, blue eyes, and high cheekbones. However, Mr. Darcy looked nothing like Lady Anne, and, therefore, must favor his father. As if she had been reading her mind, Georgiana confirmed that the black hair, gray-green eyes, and strong chin were traits of the Darcys.

"When people tell me that I look just like my mother, they can pay me no greater compliment," Georgiana said, and Lizzy nodded her head in agreement. "But I am very glad that ladies no longer powder their hair. And those enormous hats! It is amazing that they could hold their heads up."

The room was a Georgian masterpiece, decorated in soft greens with neoclassical embellishments of urns and flora centered in the picture-framed panels. The French doors led to a balcony with a view of the gardens and the woods beyond, and in the far corner of the vista was a petite Roman temple, the focal point of the garden that Lady Anne had loved best.

"Does it suit you, Elizabeth?"

"How could it not?" Lizzy said overwhelmed by all that she had seen.

"I have instructed Mrs. Reynolds to have a light supper prepared for us, and after you have rested, I will give you a brief tour of the manor house, if that is agreeable?" and Georgiana left Lizzy to her musings.

Once she was alone, Lizzy went to the window of her bedchamber and stepped out onto the balcony. As beautiful as the house was, it was the gardens that called to her. As a child, she had been a tomboy, spending as much time out of doors as possible, and she had built a refuge among the draped branches of the weeping willow tree and would shelter there during summer rain showers. She knew that somewhere out there in the parkland was her own acre of Eden. But when she thought of the size of the house and staff, she wondered if she could manage. What would be her relationship to her servants? And Georgiana had mentioned a lady's maid. Where did one find such a person? Too many thoughts. And because she was exhausted from her journey, she must put them aside for the time being, and she lay down on the settee and was quickly asleep.

In her dreams, Mr. Darcy came to her, and after taking her by the hand, he led her to the gardens and whispered that all this might be hers if only she would love him.

"But we have not spoken of love, Mr. Darcy."

"No, we have not—until now."

Chapter 10

Georgiana was correct when she said that Mrs. Reynolds would provide ample details about the house. There wasn't an urn or vase that did not merit some comment. The contents of every niche were discussed, and through their portraits, Elizabeth was introduced to Darcy's parents, grandparents, and distant ancestors. She viewed the painting of the handsome elder Mr. Darcy and admired a full-length portrait of his son, the current Master of Pemberley, which, to Lizzy's mind, failed to capture the essence of the man. Instead of being the head of an ancient tribe, he could just as well have been standing outside Covent Garden waiting for a hackney to take him home. But since the portrait was nearly ten years old, perhaps it was time for a new one, and Lizzy laughed at the thought that she was already spending Mr. Darcy's money.

"Miss Darcy's portrait is being painted as we speak," Mrs. Reynolds explained. "Her brother commissioned it in honor of her coming of age. I have not seen it, but I know that it will be perfect."

Yes, of course, it will be. The manor was perfect, the gardens were perfect, the Darcys were perfect. Everything was practically perfect in every way, that is, until she reached the east wing.

Georgiana could tell that Lizzy had absorbed as much detail as she could in one day and thanked Mrs. Reynolds for sharing so much of the history of the manor house. The housekeeper left without uttering another word.

"Mrs. Reynolds came to Pemberley when my mother married my father, and she knows more about the house than anyone except Will, but she can go on and on. Not everyone is interested in how Lady Anne acquired her collection of Chinese porcelains or my father his coin collection, but then she is used to conducting tours for people who know little of the Pemberley estate. Besides, I wanted to explain to you the reason for the unfinished appearance of this part of the house.

"The east wing is the most recent addition to Pemberley, but before the interiors could be finished, my mother died of childbed fever. Because of his profound grief, my father could not bear to be in these rooms and turned his attention to the gardens. Two years ago, Will suggested that, with the help of a designer, I should undertake the project. It was I who would choose the furniture and upholstery and select the fabric for the draperies, but I told him that I thought it would be best to leave it for the lady who would become the Mistress of Pemberley, and here you are. And so if you are agreeable, I would be happy to accompany you to London where we can visit all the shops and warehouses. We will have such fun!"

"Yes, great fun! Perhaps, my sister Jane could come as well. She has a real interest in furnishing houses." *Maybe her presence will conceal the fact that I have no interest in such things.* "I can hardly wait!" and wondered if that remark sounded in the least bit sincere.

Although Elizabeth had told Mr. Darcy that she would make her decision after she had returned to Hertfordshire from Pemberley. Apparently, Georgiana had decided the matter for both of them.

Chapter 11

With her concerns about Georgiana put to rest and her worries about managing such a large estate largely settled because of Pemberley's capable staff, Lizzy was leaning in favor of accepting Mr. Darcy's proposal of marriage. But before writing to Mr. Darcy to inform him of her decision, she had one more person she wished to consult.

The Reverend Daniel Kenner had been the vicar of St. Michael's, Lambton, for twenty-five years, having received the living from the elder Mr. Darcy. Lizzy had been hesitant about asking for a meeting in which it would be necessary to reveal such private matters to someone outside the family, but with Jane in Hertfordshire, there was no one else with whom she could discuss her concerns. When she arrived at the parsonage, she was greeted by Mrs. Kenner, the mother of the parson, his wife having died many years earlier, and she was immediately taken to the clergyman's study.

Dr. Kenner's deep blue eyes peeked out at her from under bushy eyebrows that mingled with his wild mane of white hair. When he took Lizzy's hand to welcome her, she realized that he was only an inch or two taller than she was, and his appearance and disposition lent an almost elf-like quality to him. With a face lined with laugh lines, Lizzy immediately liked him.

After listening to the details of Mr. Darcy's proposal and her feelings on the matter, Mr. Kenner expressed his opinion that she had already decided in favor of accepting Mr. Darcy's offer. She was merely looking for someone to tell her that she was not making a terrible mistake. It was then that he told her that her visit had not come as a complete surprise. Before leaving Pemberley, Darcy had paid a visit to the parsonage and had hinted that he was about to make an offer of marriage to some fortunate young lady. Although short on details, his purpose was clear, and here was the lady to prove it.

"I have known the Darcy family for more than three decades, long before I became vicar here at St. Michael's. I was in attendance when Anne Fitzwilliam married David Darcy. I baptized the infants, William and Georgiana. I buried their mother and consoled their father, and I watched as Fitzwilliam assumed the duties of Master of Pemberley long before he should have borne that weight. But his father was so consumed by grief over the loss of his dear wife that it quite incapacitated him. The boy was at Cambridge when a terrible flood caused a loss of life and extensive damage to property in Lambton and on the surrounding farms. Fitzwilliam left his studies to come home so that he might help the villagers and farmers because the senior Mr. Darcy did not know what to do. Things did improve with time, but these events caused Fitzwilliam to grow up very quickly.

"The weight of such responsibility, especially those regarding his sister, has greatly affected him. He can be overly serious, dour, and distant, which will cause some people to see him as cold and unfeeling. Nothing can be further from the truth."

"Mrs. Reynolds would be in complete agreement with that statement," Lizzy said. "She tells me that his servants are devoted to him and that there is not a tenant who will say a bad word against him. In these times, that is quite a compliment," and she thought of the vandalized threshing machine on a nearby farm in Hertfordshire as evidence of labor unrest in the country.

"Ah, yes, Mrs. Reynolds, who cannot say enough about her master. However, as much as it sounds like excessive praise, her statements are largely true. However, I must disagree with the housekeeper in one regard: The young master did *not* hang the moon," and the parson laughed at his own comment. "It is because he is an excellent landlord that Fitzwilliam was so opposed to Peter Grayson's scheme. So much filth would go into the stream on the north side of the property as a result of the manufactories he was proposing that it would pollute wells, kill fish, and cause irreparable harm to the livelihoods of all those people in the village who depend upon visitors to the Peak for their income."

"Mr. Darcy said nothing of the village and farms. He said he opposed the plan because the water for the gardens at Pemberley would be contaminated."

"They probably would be, but it would be an easy enough thing to remedy. There are other water sources on the property that could be tapped, but Lambton would suffer terribly. You see, here is another example of the goodness of the man. He did not mention that his primary reason in refusing to participate in Mr. Grayson's scheme was that he was acting in the interest of his tenants and the villagers.

"You may wonder why I speak so freely of the man. It is because I know that you will not repeat what is said here, and how do I know this? It is because I know Fitzwilliam Darcy, and he would only marry a woman of the finest character and that you can be trusted. I tell you these things because I can see that you are greatly troubled. You carry a heavy burden because marriage is a serious business. Fitzwilliam is asking you to bear his children, to be a sister to Georgiana, and to properly manage a great estate, but most importantly, to walk side by side with him through all of the rest of your days. That is a lot to ask of anyone. But he would not ask if he did not think you capable of such an undertaking.

"You have come to me for reassurance, and I can provide it. Fitzwilliam Darcy is one of the finest young men I know. It is true that there are times when he can be a stick in the mud, and he can pout like everyone else when he does not get his way. However, they are minor faults and are easily overlooked. It is the essence of the man that is important, and on that account, I can give you my unqualified assurances that he will treat you well. Because I believe you to be a woman of intelligence and sensibility, I shall not lecture you on what is required to have a successful marriage, but I will tell you that in the right soil, love can blossom, and Pemberley is famous for its blooms."

Chapter 12

Since it had been a week since her arrival at Pemberley, Darcy eagerly opened the letter from Elizabeth. During their separation, he had imagined that Georgiana and she would become friends even before they had arrived in Derbyshire and that his staff would allay any fears she had regarding the running of the household, so why had it taken her so long to reach a decision? It was only the excellent riding and the company of Sir Edward and his wife that had kept him from mounting his horse and riding to Pemberley during those interminable seven days.

> *Dear Mr. Darcy,*
>
> *After visiting with Georgiana, whom I find to be a delight, and after speaking to your staff and Mr. Kenner, I have decided to accept your offer of marriage and ask that you come to Pemberley for the purpose of determining how best to proceed. After the details are worked out, I shall return to Hertfordshire and prepare for our marriage and my move to*

Pemberley. I would hope that you will come to Longbourn to meet with my parents, but all of these things can be discussed once we are together.

I look forward to seeing you again. Yours, Elizabeth Bennet

P.S. Georgiana asked that I inform you that my middle name is Anne and that my mother's maiden name was Frances Gardiner. She sends her love.

A wave of relief washed over Darcy. Elizabeth *would* marry him and *would* become his wife, and then he scanned the brief missive, looking for evidence that she was content with her decision, but found little there. *Yours, Elizabeth Bennet.* Well, how else should she sign it? After all, he had signed his letter to her as *Yours, Fitzwilliam Darcy.* And then there was *Georgiana sends her love.* Of course, Elizabeth could not send *her* love because she did not love him. The fact that she had felt it necessary to visit the vicar indicated that she was still far from comfortable with her decision.

Considering the circumstances, he must be satisfied with her acceptance of his offer and not hope for too much too soon. After all, there had been a time when she had disliked him a great deal, but her enmity had changed from dislike to disinterest and from disinterest to curiosity. And he now believed that she actually liked him. Could like not become love? Should he confess that his feelings for her had changed months ago when she had appeared at Netherfield with her muddied boots and dirty petticoat in her quest to care for her ailing sister or that it had been his intention to begin a courtship with her even before he had learned of Grayson's engagement? No, considering their fractious relationship, she would never believe it. She would see it as an effort on his part to create an artificial love story. No, he must wait for her to fall in love with him. But what if she didn't? What would he do then?

Chapter 13

Darcy and Lizzy walked to a Roman temple folly that was at the heart of the upper garden. Unlike the formal French gardens below, Nature ruled here with little evidence of man's hand in the shrubbery and blooming plants. It was to this very place that Lizzy had come in the many days since her arrival at Pemberley. While sitting on its stone bench and viewing the rhododendrons that would burst into bloom in less than a month, she could easily contemplate being Mistress of Pemberley. It was only when she returned to the manor house and viewed the portraits of Mr. Darcy's imposing ancestors that her doubts returned. But she had made her decision, and Mr. Darcy sat beside her to discuss their future.

"I have written to Mr. Stone, my solicitor in London," Mr. Darcy began, "and he is forwarding to your father a copy of the marriage settlement. In it, there is a provision for a yearly allowance for you that I think he will find to be generous. You will be free to spend the money as you wish without any accountability to me. Your copy of the document should arrive by post within the week."

"Mr. Darcy, I am sure you have been generous. I did not think you would be otherwise. As to another matter, I hope you did not mind that I visited with the vicar?"

"Absolutely not. Mr. Kenner is a treasured family friend, and I was glad to hear that you sought his counsel. I have done the same on many occasions."

"He sang your praises, Mr. Darcy. With only one or two exceptions, he thinks you hung the moon."

One or two exceptions? Darcy wondered what they were, but then he realized that she was teasing him. Since this was something she delighted in doing, he would return the favor.

"So now you know who is responsible for placing that lunar orb in the various parts of the night sky. I did not mention it earlier as it might appear as if I was boasting," he said with a smile. "But despite Mr. Kenner's reassurances, I sense that you still have questions for me."

"Yes, I do. Your cook, Mrs. Bradshaw, who was gone until two days ago, has returned. She went into great detail about the social events hosted here at Pemberley and mentioned that among your guests are the Dukes of Devonshire and Rutland, and there is also a fête in the spring and a harvest ball in the autumn with more than two hundred guests. I just can't imagine...," she said, unable to finish her sentence.

"First, there will be no fête this spring. Preparations would have begun months ago for such an elaborate affair. Georgiana and I decided that because of her debut, it was best to concentrate on that epic event. I had no idea what was involved in preparing one single lady for her entrance into society. The logistics would confound Wellington," and after Lizzy chuckled at his being overwhelmed by such an event, he continued. "Besides, the fête is not an annual event; we host it about every three years. However, we do host an annual harvest festival in late August, but everything you need to know is set down in a book in great detail, and we hire people from the village to provide additional help.

"There is a reason why Mrs. Bradshaw told you of these special events. Her purpose is to overwhelm you. In that way, you will come to the conclusion that it is best to leave her kitchen to her with minimal supervision, and I suggest you do just that, at least for the first five years." After Lizzy smiled at his comment, he continued. "In her kitchen, she is an absolute monarchist with divine rights not claimed by our monarch, and you disagree with her at your peril."

"That sounds like excellent advice that I think I shall take. But I do hope that the servants will like me. Your mother and father are so fondly remembered, and they just adore Georgiana."

"The servants *will* love you. I shall see to it," Darcy said in all seriousness.

"Yes, the servants *must* love me," and Lizzy laughed at the absurdity of someone's emotions being dictated by another. "Is that because I am lovable, Mr. Darcy?"

Surprised by her question, he said nothing at first, but then answered, "Of course... Of course, you are lovable."

Because of his hesitation, Lizzy doubted the sincerity of his statement, but thanked him before moving on to a more serious subject.

"There is something else. My mother gave birth five times, and each time she presented my father with a daughter. What if I cannot provide you with an heir?"

"That is entirely out of our hands. It is Providence or Nature that decides such things."

"But if I cannot provide you with a son, all of this will be for naught, and Peter Grayson will inherit."

"I am in excellent health. Actually, I am in better physical condition than Peter, who eats a lot, exercises little," *as he does not like to sweat or wear dirty clothes.* "He also has a sweet tooth which will leave him gouty in his forties."

"And who is your heir if anything happens to Mr. Grayson?"

"My cousin, a little rascal, named, Malcolm Wimbley, who is eight years old. If he should inherit Pemberley, I can imagine the wholesale abandonment of

Lambton with the farmers fleeing the countryside in much the same way as the Romans fled before the Huns."

"My goodness! And he is only eight!"

"He was raised by his grandmother, my Aunt Marguerite, who rides astride a horse and who, on occasion, has gone into a men's club in town demanding to be served. For a time, she changed her name to Boadicea, but because so few people knew of the legend of the female leader of the Iceni tribe of ancient Britain, she changed it back to Marguerite. Under her direction, Malcolm has grown fearless."

"Well, we must do what we can to see that that Malcolm is not in a position to storm the heights of Pemberley."

As they made their way back to the manor house, Lizzy wondered if this engaging gentleman was the real Mr. Darcy or was this a performance put on for her benefit? His company, instead of providing clarity, only served to confuse her, and she wondered which one was the real Mr. Darcy.

Chapter 14

Mr. Bennet had requested Mrs. Bennet's attendance upon him in his library immediately after the midday meal, and she wondered what she could have done wrong. She had no doubt that it was a serious matter because she was rarely invited into his sanctuary, and on the few occasions when she was, the news had not been good.

"Mrs. Bennet, please close the door behind you. We have a matter of great importance to discuss."

"Mr. Bennet, I know I am over budget with the butcher, but that is only because of the length of Mr. Collins's visit. I have already spoken to Mr. Timlin, and he is quite happy to have the account settled at the end of next month."

"I wish this was about the butcher and your budget, but it is not. It is about our Lizzy. I am afraid that Lizzy and I were less than forthcoming with you about the reason for our daughter's visit to Derbyshire. It was not in response to an invitation by Miss Georgiana Darcy to see the Peak. Rather, Elizabeth went to the Darcy estate to decide if she could accept an offer of marriage from the Master of Pemberley," and Mr. Bennet proceeded to tell his wife all that had occurred with regard to Mr. Darcy.

"Mr. Darcy! I can hardly believe it. Mr. Darcy wants to marry our Lizzy? But he does not even like her," Mrs. Bennet answered in a voice filled with confusion.

"Lizzy tells me that he *does* like her, but that he is a stoic fellow and not one to show his emotions. But you sound as if you do not approve of the match. Is that true?"

"But he is so... so stern," she said, not answering the question.

"I am puzzled by your response. I thought you would have been running out the door by now to rub the news in Lady Lucas's face. There was a time when you pictured Mr. Collins marrying Elizabeth, but you seem to object to her marrying someone who is that pompous arse's superior in every way."

"But this is different. If Elizabeth had given Mr. Collins any encouragement, he might have made her an offer. But whenever he looked in her direction, Lizzy gave him such a look that I am sure the man feared that he might be turned into stone. Who would make an offer to a woman capable of such a cold gesture?"

"Mrs. Bennet, you digress," her husband said, tapping the desk with his finger.

"What I am saying is that because Lizzy is so very clever things would have worked out with Mr. Collins. It would have been no time at all before she would have had Mr. Collins doing her bidding, and he would have been all the better for it as she would have drummed some sense into his wooden head. But Mr. Darcy. Oh, no! He will not do anyone's bidding. Is she resolved to do this?"

"Apparently so. In this morning's post I received a letter from Mr. Stone, the Darcy solicitor, enclosing the marriage contract. It was mailed to me at Mr. Darcy's direction, and so it appears that our dear girl has agreed to become Mrs. Darcy."

"Well, if she is resolved to do it, we cannot stop her. She is a headstrong girl."

"Yes, we know her too well. She will not be talked out of it," and Mr. Bennet let out a sigh of resignation.

Mrs. Bennet, unsettled by the unexpected news, rose to leave, but her husband asked her to sit down again.

"Fanny, I owe you an apology. For the life of me, I could not understand your enthusiasm for a possible match between Mr. Collins and Lizzy, but now I know that you *had* thought it through. In your mind, you had imagined those two very different people coming to some sort of accommodation and living together in harmony if not in love. I did not give you enough credit."

"Tom, I know that Lizzy is your favorite child and that you have always hoped that she would marry for love, as did I. But it was never really in the stars, now was it? Between the lack of a dowry and her fondness for her own opinions, it was not likely that a suitor would come forward. So I thought that if she married your cousin, at least she would have her own household and would have more say in the running of it than most wives can boast of upon entering the marriage state. Although the entail was never far from my mind, my primary purpose in promoting the match with her was to secure a future for Elizabeth. She is also my daughter, and I do love her."

"Of course, my dear. Again, my apologies."

"Well, when she returns, we must do our best to be full of good cheer. Lord knows that she will need it."

Chapter 15

For the next week, Mr. Darcy and his sister did all that they could to acquaint Elizabeth with the responsibilities of being the Mistress of Pemberley. In addition to daily consultations with Mrs. Bradshaw and Mrs. Reynolds, it would be necessary for Lizzy to know all the tenants who leased their farms from Mr. Darcy. She would also be required to frequent the shops of the merchants in Lambton and to visit with Mr. Kenner so that she would be aware of the needs of the less fortunate of the parish.

That was just the beginning of the tutorial. It was a Darcy tradition to attend as many local festivities as possible and to be aware of marriages, births, and deaths of their neighbors. She would also need to establish a correspondence with their more exalted neighbors, the Devonshires and Rutlands, as well as members of the gentry. There were discussions on entertaining in the country as well as in town, what her responsibilities would be during the London season, people she needed to become acquainted with and those to be avoided, the etiquette required in matters of precedence, and how to address those superior to her in rank. With all the information that she was being fed, Lizzy thought that her head would come off her shoulders like a child's spinning top.

Despite references to members of the aristocracy and dances at the finest venues in London, the biggest concern for Lizzy remained the servants. She had gone below stairs on two occasions, and after walking the corridors and peeking into the work areas, she understood that she was to be the head of a virtual army of parlor and laundry maids, kitchen workers, grooms, etc. At Longbourn, Mr. and Mrs. Hill, although in the Bennets' employ, were considered to be family, but that would not be the case at Pemberley.

"The relationship you have with the Hills will not work on such a large estate," Mr. Darcy had told her. "Except on the most important of occasions, such as during Yuletide, you will rarely see those who work in the scullery, dairy, stable, coach house, or the laundry, and because Mrs. Reynolds does her job so well, you should not see a parlor maid at work. However, if a female servant finds herself in difficulty, your advice and assistance will be sought. Fortunately, that is a rare event at Pemberley because we employ the sons and daughters of tenant farmers who have been raised in the church and who make sure their children understand the benefits of working here as we are generous with our wages."

Despite all the information and reassurances that he was providing, Darcy could see that Elizabeth was still unsettled, possibly more so than when they had begun.

"It will take some getting used to, but you will eventually establish your own routine and manner of doing things, and, remember, you will choose your own lady's maid, so you will have someone with you whenever you wish. But even then, you must be very careful as servants will talk, and gossip provides fodder for the newspapers and pamphleteers."

To put Lizzy at her ease, Mr. Darcy reassured her that everyone at Pemberley was there to help her succeed and that his mother had undergone a similar experience when she had arrived in Derbyshire.

"My mother was only eighteen years old when she came to Pemberley as a new bride, and in those days, Derbyshire was much more of a wilderness. The roads were terrible, and travel was extremely difficult. But that is no longer the case. As lord of the manor, it is my responsibility to see that the roads are kept in good repair, and I do. Derbyshire is no longer a wilderness, and you have the advantage of three years on my mother. You will be a bride at twenty-one, not eighteen."

But your mother's father was an earl and her mother a countess, and she had been in training to be the mistress of such a house for her entire life, Lizzy mused, but remained silent.

All matters were presented by the master in a businesslike manner because it was a business—the business of marriage. *But I shall put my shoulder to the wheel, and do this, and, eventually, it will become second nature.* Or so she hoped.

* * *

The first of the banns were announced at St. Michael's on the day before their departure to Hertfordshire, and because Elizabeth and Mr. Darcy, had been in and out of the shops hinting at an engagement, a murmur of approval was heard cascading through the church. Everyone who had met Lizzy liked her, and they were so profuse in their praise of their Darcy neighbors that she was beginning to think that her betrothed really had hung the moon. And she found that her opinion of the man improved with each day to the point where any feelings she had held against him were melting away as snow in spring.

By the time Elizabeth, Georgiana, and Mr. Darcy were on the road to Longbourn, all of the details of the marriage had been worked out, and she had written a lengthy letter to her parents informing them of her arrival at Longbourn. The letter also indicated that they would be staying in Hertfordshire for only two weeks before returning to Pemberley with Jane and Charles.

Mr. Darcy, who was aware that Mr. Bennet had been cool to the arrangement, was on edge during the journey to Hertfordshire. Whenever he had thought about such things, Darcy had always assumed that his future father-in-law would be pleased with the match. After all, he was universally regarded as an "excellent catch." At least that was the opinion of the editors of *The Insider* as well as the writers of the scandal sheets, to say nothing of his sister. But in all his imaginings, he had not conjured up the present scenario. It had never occurred to him that his wife's family would not like him. But Mr. Bennet's tepid approval of the match was nothing compared to the fact that he was marrying a woman who did not love him.

Chapter 16

As the carriage once again traveled north towards Pemberley following their visit to Longbourn, Jane, Georgiana, and Elizabeth shared stories of their childhood. Lizzy and Jane spoke of their being inseparable all through their youth. Because Lizzy was a tomboy and Jane was most definitely not, many of the stories centered on the adventures that Lizzy had dreamt up, most of which involved crawling behind some bush or rock and getting wet in Longbourn's pond. It was all great fun, and Georgiana giggled in delight.

Of course, Miss Darcy's upbringing had been one of privilege, where few wishes went unfulfilled. Although there had been time set aside to play with her dolls in a large dollhouse on the estate or to toss a ball to her much older brother, her free time was limited as her days were filled with practicing on the pianoforte, singing lessons, dancing masters, French and Italian tutors, and learning all the arts expected of a lady who would move in the top tier of society. Lizzy did not begrudge her such a childhood. She was quite content that she had been allowed to make mud pies rather than having to learn how to speak Italian.

While the girls enjoyed sharing golden memories, a second carriage, containing Mr. Darcy and Mr. Bingley, traveled behind them, but the conversation was anything but lively. Although Darcy was to be married in a few short days, he was burdened by the knowledge that at Longbourn everything had been turned on its head. Instead of the Bennets delighting in the excellent match their daughter had made, Mr. Bennet looked as if he were attending a funeral. Even Mrs. Bennet, who appeared to be more confused than pleased, had little to say. But that did not mean that while Lizzy had been in Derbyshire, Elizabeth's mother had sat idle.

After giving the matter considerable thought, Mrs. Bennet had seen that the benefits of the match far outweighed its disadvantages, and she had smoothed Lizzy's way in Meryton and amongst her neighbors, praising Mr. Darcy's friendship with Mr. Bingley, portraying him as a doting older brother, mentioning his kindness to Jane and Charles in providing his seaside villa for their honeymoon, and hinting at the most generous marriage settlement that anyone could possibly hope for. Although she could not mention the particulars, what would one expect from a man who had £10,000 a year and very likely more? As a result, when the newly-engaged couple walked down Meryton's High Street, they were met by well-wishers and smiles. If only that had been the case with the family.

Following the announcement, Jane and Mary found that they could manage little more than weak smiles whenever the couple looked their way. Mr. Bingley did his best to add some cheer to the somber group by proposing a toast. Although everyone drank to the couple's health, the levity that had greeted Jane and Charles's engagement was lacking. It was only Lydia and Kitty who offered their sincere congratulations, but all their merriment ceased when Elizabeth informed them that the marriage ceremony would be a small affair at St. Michael's in Lambton with only Charles, Jane, and Miss Darcy in attendance. For Lizzy, the thought of her disapproving father witnessing her nuptials was too painful to contemplate and was something best avoided.

"No wedding dress or wedding breakfast, Lizzy?" Kitty asked followed by a disappointed Lydia who saw her dreams of an elaborate wedding with musicians and dancing, and one in which she would serve as a bridesmaid, evaporate, only to be replaced by the knowledge that all she was getting out of this whole affair was the dour Mr. Darcy as a brother-in-law.

Darcy only knew the half of it. After seeing the man to the door, Mr. Bennet had called his daughter into the study where the conversation had been less than cordial.

"Have no fear, Lizzy. I have not withdrawn my consent," a distressed Mr. Bennet had told her. "Mr. Darcy is the kind of man to whom I should never dare refuse anything. But please keep in mind that although he is now bound to you and cannot break this engagement without injuring his reputation, you, on the other hand, are free to rid yourself of this millstone that you have placed around your neck."

"Papa, please."

"My dear, before you do this, I wish you to know that economies can be made, and we are by no means without resources."

Lizzy merely shook her head. Her father had been encouraging her mother to economize for nearly twenty-five years without success, and his habits of expense were little better than hers. As for family savings, a modest sum had been set aside so that Mrs. Bennet would have something to live on in the event Mr. Collins, upon the death of Mr. Bennet, exercised his right under the entail and asked the family to leave Longbourn. The only way for Lizzy to provide financial security for her family was to proceed with the wedding

"I have come to ask you for your blessing on my marriage to Mr. Darcy."

"Bless a loveless match? I shall not. That man has turned you into a brood mare."

Lizzy's eyes filled with tears. "How can you say such a thing? This happens all the time amongst royalty and the aristocracy and even the gentry. It was such an arranged marriage that brought our sovereigns together. Would you call Queen Charlotte a brood mare?"

Upon seeing his daughter's tears, a remorseful Mr. Bennet said, "My child, I am so sorry."

"Papa, I am begging you to refrain from saying anything like that ever again as it truly pains me. It will do no good, but it can do great harm. You must believe me when I say that Mr. Darcy is good and kind. His vicar told me that the Darcys are so generous to their servants that they are criticized by their neighbors for paying such high wages, and then there are the improvements he has made to the cottages and on his property for the benefit of his tenants. When I walked in Lambton on his arm, all the shopkeepers came out to greet him and shared all of the latest news about their businesses and families, and he knew every one of them by name. By going to Pemberley, I saw an entirely different Mr. Darcy from the gentleman who would not dance with me at the assembly. I can say with absolute certainty that my first impressions of Mr. Darcy were wrong."

"Lizzy, that is all well and good. But the fact is that Mr. Darcy does not love you."

"Do you think I do not know that? But it is my hope that in the future that he will come to love me for myself and not just because I am the mother of his children."

"I pray that it is so. But Lizzy, you do not love him either."

Lizzy made no comment, but Mr. Bennet could see from the set of her jaw and the look in her eyes that she would not be talked out of it. With nothing more to be done, Mr. Bennet kissed his beloved daughter and gave her his blessing.

Chapter 17

The day of her wedding had arrived, and Lizzy and Jane looked out the window at the dreary scene before them. Three days of rain had been succeeded by a fog that rose out of the landscape like vapors escaping from an erupting caldera. The gardens, which afforded Lizzy so much pleasure, were obscured, and only the barest outline of the giant oaks that shaded the property could be seen. The bride arrived at the church wearing her pelisse and brown boots, which were quickly removed, to be replaced by ivory satin slippers. Because the old stone church was cold, she could feel the chill of the slate through her slippers, and she began to shiver, but was unsure if it was because of the cold or her impending wedding ceremony.

Rather than buy a new dress, Lizzy had chosen to wear Jane's. But because it was March, lace sleeves were added, and in order to make it her own creation, cream-colored rosettes were sewn on the hem and tiny pearls added to the bodice. Around her neck was a cross made of opal that Fitzwilliam's mother had worn when she had married David Darcy, and Georgiana had presented Lizzy with a beautiful mantilla made of Venetian lace as her gift to the bride.

Elizabeth's appearance at the rear of the church took Darcy's breath away. She was so beautiful, and he must tell her so. And he loved her, but he could not tell her that—not yet. But he would take his vows to love, honor, and cherish her seriously—starting today. And he smiled broadly, and his happy visage reassured Lizzy that all would be well.

As she stood beside him at the altar, Darcy could tell that she was freezing, and he took a step closer to her so that the sleeve of his coat touched her arm, and she looked at him and nodded her thanks. As soon as they were pronounced man and wife, Darcy asked Charles to fetch "Mrs. Darcy's pelisse," and it was that statement, more than anything, that brought home the truth of what had just happened. She truly was Mrs. Fitzwilliam Darcy, and it was further reinforced as the newlyweds signed the registry.

While the couple had been exchanging vows, the skies had opened up for a brief but heavy shower, and Lizzy looked down at her thin satin slippers and realized that she would have to change back into her ugly brown boots, but before she could do so, Mr. Darcy swooped her up into his arms and carried her to the waiting carriage. After he had returned to the church to provide the same service for his sister, Charles, who was laughing heartily, duplicated the exercise with Jane. It was the perfect conclusion to the somber service, and they were still laughing when the carriage arrived at Pemberley.

Knowing that the staff would be waiting for her at the manor house, Lizzy had no wish to be carried across the threshold in view of dozens of servants, and so she reluctantly put on her boots, and her sister and sister-in-law did the same. At the house, Mr. Jackson and three grooms armed with umbrellas were waiting, and the wedding party was escorted into the main hall where they were greeted by parallel lines of servants in starched white uniforms or the Darcy livery. Jackson introduced each of the servants, but Lizzy was too nervous to remember their names. In time, she would make it a point to get to know all of them. But at the end of the line were a few familiar faces: Mrs. Reynolds, Mrs. Brotherton, Mr. Ferguson, the gardener, and the imperious Mrs. Bradshaw.

In honor of their wedding day, Elizabeth had arranged with Jackson for the distribution of monies from her personal account to each of the servants. In her first act of defiance, Lizzy refused to yield when Mrs. Bradshaw had told her that she was being overly generous and that such a gesture would make the staff think that they could take advantage of their new mistress. But she had refused to listen, explaining that such a momentous event demanded a dramatic gesture.

After the servants were dismissed, the small party adjourned to the dining room where a sumptuous wedding feast had been prepared, but Lizzy had no appetite, and she consumed only a few spoonfuls of soup and a slice of bread at the insistence of her husband, who was doing his best to settle her nerves. The evening was a combination of cards, music, and dancing, and all truly enjoyed themselves. Lizzy was quite relaxed because with Jane's encouragement, she had imbibed three glasses of wine and was feeling rather tipsy, a new experience for her. But the evening came to an end when Georgiana announced that she wished to retire and Charles declared that he was ready for his bed. Unfortunately, Lizzy was not ready for hers.

* * *

Right or left side? Lizzy wondered as she stared at the bed. *Left side. Definitely.* Mr. Darcy's bedchamber was to the right, so it made sense for her to sleep on the left, and she quickly climbed into the enormous bed. When she heard the door open, her heart started pounding, and it continued to beat so hard that it was echoing in her head. Once in bed beside her, Mr. Darcy took her hand and gently squeezed it and asked her if she had had a nice day.

"Yes, sir. It was quite pleasant, and you looked very handsome."

"And you were extraordinarily beautiful. But I think now that we are man and wife, something less formal than 'sir' might be in order. You may call me William, or do as Georgiana does, and call me Will. Only my Aunt Catherine refers to me as Fitzwilliam."

"Yes, William." *Not Will, not yet. Too informal, which is strange considering that we are in bed together.*

"Was everything to your satisfaction?" William asked.

"Up to this point, yes. I mean, I don't know what is… Yes, everything was fine."

Darcy smiled at her, and after putting his arm around her shoulder, he pulled her to him, but after burying his head in her neck, everything that followed was a blur. Lizzy could feel her chemise being lifted, his full weight upon her, and then a searing pain. Biting her lip to keep from crying out, Lizzy could think of nothing but the pain until it suddenly stopped, and her husband rolled on to his side. The two lay together in the dark for several minutes, but not so much as a word was uttered. *What could possibly be said after such a loveless exercise*, Lizzy thought? After kissing her on her cheek, her husband whispered that he hoped that she would be happy in her new home, and following another few minutes of silence, he left.

Lizzy lay staring at the satin canopy, the flickering candlelight making waves of the pleated fabric above her, her brain barely comprehending what had just happened. But with a lingering pain between her legs and the empty space next to her where her husband should have been, reality descended. *He left as soon as he could; he didn't even want to sleep with me.* And the tenderness that she had felt growing in her bosom from the time of her first visit to Pemberley was not enough to ease the heartache she was experiencing. Pulling her legs up to her chest, she buried her head in the pillow to muffle the sound of her sobs.

* * *

"Damn! That went badly," Darcy said out loud. "I hurt her. I know I did. She was not ready. I should have known that she would not be." Darcy knew how to make love to a woman, but he had never had sexual congress with a maiden and had failed to anticipate that her body needed preparation.

"But what was I to do? Because she does not love me, she would have thought me a brute if I had caressed her as I would have wished. But this is not acceptable. I cannot inflict pain on my wife." Darcy pounded the bed in frustration. He wondered what would have happened if she had invited him to stay with her for the night. A second time would have been less of a shock and, hopefully, less painful. But she had said nothing, leaving him with no choice but to return to his own bedchamber.

"I was right to leave, wasn't I?" Darcy asked the two whippets sitting at his feet. "Because if Elizabeth had wanted me to stay, she would have said as much or indicated by some gesture that she wished for me to remain. Instead, she lay beside me as if a statute," and the memory of her gasp when he had entered her and her shallow breathing served as proof of just how badly it had gone. "But these things take time, and with each visit, things will be easier. Maybe there will come a time when she will truly want me to stay." But after remembering the coldness of their brief encounter, he doubted it would be anytime soon.

Chapter 18

While Lizzy was performing her morning toilette, Jane came to visit. After dismissing the servant, Jane asked her sister if she was all right.

"I am fine. Everything was fine," Lizzy answered with as much enthusiasm as she could muster.

But from the look on Lizzy's face, Jane very much doubted that everything was just fine. "Did it hurt?" Jane boldly asked.

"A little. But from our conversations, I had expected as much."

"Was it easier the second time?"

The second time? "There was no second time. It had been a long day for both of us, and we were very tired," Lizzy answered truthfully. She saw no reason to tell her sister that there could be no second time when your husband was not in the same room with you.

"That was very thoughtful of him. I must confess that I had not planned for a repeat performance during the night or the third time when morning arrived. It came as quite a surprise to me." Jane spoke of these personal matters because she wanted Lizzy to know that no matter how thoughtful Mr. Darcy was, he was still a man, and she could hardly expect a newly married man to be "thoughtful" on more than the first night. "I predict the second time will be easier, but you can help it along if you are better prepared."

"Prepared? But how?"

"I know that you do not love Mr. Darcy, but is it possible for you to pretend that you do? Can you imagine welcoming his kisses? Because if you do, there is a change that takes place within, and it will be much easier for you. Eventually, you may even come to enjoy it. So my suggestion is that before Mr. Darcy comes to you tonight that you picture the scene of your coming together as a pleasurable event, and you will be surprised by what happens."

Lizzy nodded, but she had no idea what Jane was talking about. She was no longer a virgin, except in the matter of kisses.

* * *

Elizabeth was the last person to come into the breakfast room, and all had been waiting for her before preparing their plates. Darcy immediately jumped up, and after greeting his wife, offered to butter a piece of toast for her.

"Thank you, Mr. Darcy. I mean William, that would be very nice."

With everyone watching her, she declared that she had slept well and that her bed was more than comfortable. "It was the same as sleeping on a cloud," and everyone smiled at her description.

"Elizabeth, I was mentioning to Jane and Charles that there is an exceptional view of the Peak about four miles from here," her husband said. "Because there are no leaves on the trees, there is a long view of the valley that is hidden for most of the year. Would you care to ride up there in the barouche? It is an easy drive."

"Of course. I would love to see any part of the Peak."

Although the rain had stopped and the fog had lifted, the day was cold, and with the sun putting in an infrequent appearance, it was necessary for the five tourists to huddle under blankets. Darcy sat between his sister and Elizabeth and used the cold as an excuse to pull his wife closer to him. Lizzy could feel his leg pressed against hers and his hand brushing against her thigh, and she felt a physical change that she could not explain, except that it was very pleasant. Maybe this was what Jane had been talking about.

Despite the cold, the day was perfectly lovely. For twelve hours, Lizzy did not have to think about her conjugal responsibilities. She only hoped that tonight would not be a repeat of her wedding night. As she waited for Mr. Darcy to come to her bedchamber, she pictured their time together in the barouche. But in her imagination, he moved his hand up and down her thigh, and the pleasant sensation returned. The only person more relieved than Lizzy by this physical change was Mr. Darcy, who found their second time together to be infinitely superior to their first. He entered her with no effort and found the woman beneath him to be more lifelike than the wooden board of the previous night. But the question remained: would she ask him to stay? As he lay in the dark, with his hand brushing against hers, he bided his time, waiting to hear the words that she wished him to remain. But again, she said nothing. Without her permission to spend the night, he felt that he must return to his own bedchamber.

"Small steps," he said as soon as he had closed the door to their adjoining rooms. "That is what is needed here. Small steps. Tonight was much better than last night, and tomorrow will be better yet." After drifting off to sleep, Elizabeth came to him in his dreams, and with a passion that had been denied him in real life, he made love to his wife in a union in which she was fully engaged.

* * *

Each passing day was the same as the one before: days filled with enjoyable excursions and entertainments and nights all about the business of producing an heir. But on the sixth day, it was necessary for the Bingleys to leave as Charles's younger brother was to be married in London, and they were expected to attend the ceremony. Lizzy and Jane had a tearful goodbye, but Lizzy assured her sister that her husband was a kind man and that she would be fine.

"Besides, Georgiana and I get along famously, and I am comforted by the fact that I do have someone to talk to." What went unsaid was that she wished it was her husband with whom she could converse. But shortly after they had completed the act of procreation, he returned to his own room. Each and every night.

But with her beloved sister gone, Lizzy felt an overwhelming sense of isolation, and she needed reassurance that William cared for her. She understood that he was not in love with her, but surely after a week, he felt something—some kernel of affection—because she certainly did. And that night, when she felt his weight upon her, she moved willingly beneath him, and when she felt his surge nearing, she wrapped her legs around his and pulled him into her depths. After the final thrust, she could feel his heart pounding as he lay quietly on top of her.

As he had done on every other night, he stood beside the bed, and she expected that he would make some superficial comment about what activity awaited them in the morning. But this time, he wore a look of confusion and said nothing. Lizzy returned his look, praying that he would say something, but the man remained silent. Finally, with neither saying anything, Darcy bowed and left, and Elizabeth was so frustrated that eyeing the vase on the mantle, she pictured it sailing through the air, crashing against his door. She was not alone in her frustration.

Once he was behind closed doors, Darcy poured a stiff drink. "What the devil was that all about? Did we make love or not? No, you have to be in love to make love. But Elizabeth *did* enjoy it. I know she did, and yet, she did not ask me to stay. Why? Are we now about to embark on a physical relationship devoid of love?" And the thought sickened him. "This cannot go on. Something has to change. Tomorrow, I will confess my love to her and hope that she can love me in return." And he felt tears forming. "Oh God! What have I done?"

Chapter 19

Lizzy did not think she could be more hurt than she had been the previous night when Mr. Darcy had left her after she had willingly given herself to him. With her looks, she had done everything except beg him to stay with her, and although he had stared right at her, he had left anyway, but this time, without a word. She had willingly yielded every fiber of her being, and it had been wonderful! She felt as if for the first time that they had come together as man and wife, not two strangers ensuring the continuation of a dynasty, and she felt something stir inside her that could only mean that she had fallen in love with her husband. But then he had withdrawn. And that stare! To be looked at in such a way and then to turn his back on her! She was humiliated.

Lizzy did not as yet know the depth of her humiliation. When she went down to breakfast, she learned from Georgiana that using the excuse of visiting tenants on the far side of the property, her brother was already gone from the house. "He will not return before dark."

Good grief! Was it necessary for him to run away? Is this is his way of punishing me for showing some feeling for him? But I cannot rebuke him. He gave me his reasons for marrying me, and I accepted the conditions. So be it. If this is how it is to be, I shall have a heart of stone. I shall not let him hurt me again.

Fortunately, the weather was fine, and Georgiana and Lizzy spent most of the day in the gardens. Lizzy had sought out Mr. Ferguson to discuss the spring blooms. With her dreary interior life, she needed to see the colors of Nature so that it might lift her spirits.

"Ma'am, everything is just about ready to go," the old gardener said. "If you look closely, you'll see that the flowers are about to start budding. You've got to be patient a bit longer, but it'll be worth the wait. I've got some pretty ones already blooming in the greenhouse. They're the ones I send up to the house for the centerpieces. Would you like some of those?"

"Thank you, Mr. Ferguson, but I would prefer to see them in their natural state," and Lizzy left the man to his work.

* * *

Mr. Darcy joined the ladies for supper, but Lizzy showed no interest in any subject broached by her husband or his sister, and she had no appetite whatsoever. Finally, citing fatigue, she asked to be excused.

"Good night, Georgiana. William, I shall see you later tonight." She turned and departed.

Darcy knew enough about women to know that there were times in the month when it was best to leave them alone. Perhaps, this was Elizabeth's time.

"Georgiana, would you mind seeing if Elizabeth is all right?"

"I would gladly do so, Will, but I think she needs you, not me."

"Why? Do you think she is upset with me? I mean, I have been gone all day. What could I have possibly done?"

"I do not know, but I still think that it would be best if you went and found out."

As Darcy raised his hand to knock on the door, Elizabeth's personal servant was coming out of her mistress's bedchamber, and he could glimpse his wife at her dressing table brushing her hair.

"May I come in, Elizabeth?"

"It is your house. You may go wherever you wish."

"Are you ill?"

"I am perfectly well. But if I did feel ill, there are servants to see to my needs. You need not concern yourself."

"But I am concerned," he said, and his heart ached at the sight of her obvious unhappiness with him.

"Really, Mr. Darcy? You are concerned?" She felt the tears welling up in her eyes. "I know that you do not love me, but was it necessary for you to go to the far reaches of your property so that you might not see me today? And why was I treated thusly? Because I demonstrated some affection for you last night? But please do not worry. I shall not do any such thing again. You have my promise," Lizzy said with tears pouring down her cheeks, and she turned away from him and walked to the bed.

"You misunderstand me."

"*I* misunderstand *you*? I think not. It is quite clear that you do not want me, except to give birth to your heir."

"Not want you? It is *you* who does not want *me*!"

"How dare you say such a thing!" she said, turning on him. "Last night, when I pulled you inside me or when I held you close to me or when I looked into your eyes before you left, pleading with you to stay, are those signs of someone who does not want you?"

"Then why did you not say something? Because I cannot stay without your permission, night after night, I have waited for you to ask me to stay. But I *wanted* to stay so very much… because I love you."

When Lizzy heard those words, she knew that she would strike out at him. "Do not say words you do not mean because you think I want to hear them," she said, pounding his chest. "I hate lies more than anything.

Please do not lie to me," she said, collapsing into his arms.

Darcy kissed the top of her head. "I am not lying, my dearest Elizabeth. I *do* love you, but I confess that I am guilty of the sin of omission."

"What? What are you saying?" she asked, drying her tears on the sleeve of her dressing gown.

"When I asked you to marry me, I mentioned your honesty as my sole reason for placing you above all others, and it is a virtue that I prize greatly. However, it was certainly not the only reason I asked you to marry me. Elizabeth, I have been in love with you since you came to Netherfield on that rainy day with the hem of your dress six inches deep in mud, your boots filthy, your gorgeous hair wild, and your amazing eyes ablaze. But I would be lying now if I told you that I did not fight against those feelings because I considered you to be my inferior. But you are not. You are better than me. You are good and kind, and you would never have lied to me."

Lizzy looked at her husband, and when she did, she saw love. For the first time, she saw love.

"But why did you run away today?"

"I was not running from you, but toward you. I have spent the whole of this day trying to figure out how best to tell you how much I love you. Knowing that your feelings did not match my own, I was prepared to say that I will not abandon hope of your loving me someday—that I will shower you with so much affection that, in the end, you must give way under the weight of it and fall in love with me."

"Oh, William! You certainly have my permission to shower me with affection," Lizzy said, "but I have something to confess as well. I too have committed the sin of omission."

"What do you mean?" Darcy asked with hope in his voice.

"I have not told you of my feelings for you. I love *you*, William" and she started to cry all over again.

After drying her tears with his handkerchief, he asked, "Are you sure? You are not just saying that?" Lizzy shook her head "no." "But when did you fall in love with me?"

"I think I had the first inkling at the Netherfield ball," she answered. "When you tried so hard to converse with me, but no matter the subject, I refused to give you a reasonable answer. But you kept trying anyway. Even though I could see how much I aggravated you, you would not give up. And then when we danced together at Jane and Charles's wedding, I felt such strong feelings for you. But it was an impossibility, wasn't it? The Darcys of the world do not marry the Elizabeth Bennets of the world."

"Except that they do. Elizabeth, please forgive me," and he placed both hands on her face and pulled her to him, and for the first time, their lips touched in a deep and abiding exchange of love, and it was enough to ignite the passion that had been stirring within both of them. They were soon in bed, and that night they learned the physical side of being in love.

Chapter 20

"Will, you really must let me go," Lizzy said, fighting to free herself from his arms. "It is gone half past ten. What will your sister think?"

"Georgie will think that I love my wife, and that we have decided to spend the day together in bed."

"Spend the day in bed?" Lizzy said in full blush. "I could never. Everyone would think that we were..."

"Making love."

Lizzy tried once again to get out of bed, but her husband would not release her. "Will, I do not think I could. Honestly, you will wear me out, and I shall have to refuse you tonight."

"But we have to make up for lost time. You told me last night that Jane and Charles made love three times on their wedding night. Since you and I have been married for eight nights, we should have made love twenty-four times. So we have to make love thirteen more times in order to catch up with the Bingleys."

"Whatever possessed me to tell you that?" Lizzy asked, shaking her head.

"Let that be a warning to you. Unlike many husbands, I pay attention to what my wife says."

"I am happy to hear it, so please listen now. You are going to go back to your room. Do not shake your head 'no.' I *must* see to my toilette. Now go, and if breakfast is still being served, I shall see you at breakfast."

Lizzy was practically dancing on air. During the night, when William and she were not making love, they were telling each other how much they loved each other, one trying to outdo the other in the depth of their affection. With the knowledge that William had been in love with her for months, Lizzy looked at everything with different eyes, and because of it, the memories changed. The sting went out of his looks and the bite out of his words.

While Mercer laid out his master's clothes, Darcy was humming. It was music to the servant's ears. The hastily arranged marriage had not gone well, and Mercer had guessed that Mr. Darcy's feelings for his wife were not reciprocated. But this morning, his master's joyful countenance indicated otherwise, and he knew that for the first time that Mr. Darcy had spent the entire night with his bride. Whatever the misunderstanding had been, it had been cleared up, and he started to hum as well.

Although there was clarity on the first floor of Pemberley, Georgiana was confused. She had been waiting for the newlyweds in the breakfast room, but neither had appeared. She was especially eager to see them because she had heard Elizabeth's sobs coming from their room the previous evening. But here was Lizzy, all smiles. In fact, she looked happier than at any time since becoming Mrs. Fitzwilliam Darcy.

"Good morning, Georgiana. It is a beautiful day, is it not?" Lizzy asked without looking out the window. "Oh, I see that it is raining, but no matter, it is still a beautiful day."

"'Beauty in things exists merely in the mind which contemplates them,' or so Dr. Hume said, and if you think it is a beautiful day, then it is," Georgiana said, smiling, but then she adopted a more serious countenance. "Elizabeth, I want you to know that I love you as a sister, and I want you to be happy here."

"I *am* happy. I promise you that I am."

"But last night, I heard..."

"Oh, I am sorry that you heard us quarrel. But that was last night, and everything has changed. Your brother and I declared our love for each other as if we were standing before the vicar once again. So loud voices were replaced by soft utterances, and all harsh words are forthwith banished from the halls of Pemberley. Or at least until your brother annoys me again."

"Well, that will never happen as I cannot have you distressing my sister," Darcy said as he entered the room, and after squeezing his sister's hand, he placed a firm kiss on his wife's cheek, and Lizzy looked at him with so much love that Georgiana was reassured that all was well at Pemberley.

Chapter 21

"Tom, I know that it is difficult for you to believe that Lizzy can be happy with 'such a man.' But we have now had three letters from her, and it is quite obvious to *most* of her family that she is quite content to be Mrs. Darcy," Mrs. Bennet said in a scolding voice.

"Fanny, if you choose to believe that our daughter somehow in the space of one month developed an affection for a man who only married her so that he might have an heir, you should do so. But I refuse to be deceived."

Mrs. Bennet took out the latest letter from Pemberley:

Dear Family,

I hope this letter finds all of you in good health. I am well and in excellent spirits. Mr. Darcy treats me as if I were a princess, and I awake each morning with the satisfaction of knowing that my husband loves me dearly and that I love him as well. As I had mentioned in my earlier letters, I did not think it would be so. But Fortune has truly shined upon me, and I find that I am in a union where love and respect grows daily. I could not be happier…

"Of course, Lizzy would write that. She does not want us to worry about her," Mr. Bennet said, continuing to insist that his daughter could not possibly be content with such a disagreeable person.

"Well, you will have an opportunity to judge for yourself as they are coming to Hertfordshire. Miss Darcy is to make her debut this season, and they are on their way to London to visit the shops. And although they will stay with Charles and Jane, I am reasonably sure that they will make time for us as well, that is, if they are not met by frowns and disapproving looks from a certain member of the family."

If Mr. Bennet doubted what he had read or could not agree with what he had heard from his wife, there was no way he could deny what was right before his eyes. In the five weeks since he had last seen his Lizzy, his daughter had blossomed into a beautiful mature woman, and it was obvious that she loved her husband very much. Seeing the looks exchanged between the newlyweds, it was impossible for Mr. Bennet to hold to the belief that Mr. Darcy did not love his daughter. The look on Darcy's face was such that it reminded him of a young man, who twenty-five years earlier, had looked on the golden-haired daughter of the local solicitor and had fallen in love at first sight.

"Lizzy, may I see you in my study? Alone."

Elizabeth followed her father into his sanctuary, and there she reassured him that she was truly and profoundly in love with her husband.

"I do love him. I truly do. And I understand your concerns and that is because you do not know him, not yet, but when you do, you will come to admire him. Indeed, he has no improper pride. He is amiable and perfectly suited for me."

"Well, my dear, I have no more to say. If this be the case, he deserves you."

"Then let us celebrate. You were not at our wedding, and our betrothal was less than a joyous occasion. So may we begin again?"

"I would like nothing better," and he kissed his daughter, and knowing that she would be living in faraway Derbyshire, tears came to his eyes. But he was consoled in knowing that the tears he shed were tears of joy. His Lizzy was truly happy.

Chapter 22

On the day before her departure for Hertfordshire, Lizzy had spent a good part of the day wandering about Pemberley's gardens. The buds were about to open, and she regretted that she would not be here to see them in their first bloom. But Georgiana must be in London to prepare for her coming out and that took precedence, and there would be many springs at Pemberley to enjoy.

That evening, after supper, she found Will in his study pouring over the estate accounts, but as soon as he saw his bride, he put his pen down.

"Come in, Elizabeth. I am just about finished. Mr. Aiken keeps such excellent accounts that there is little for me to do but sign my name to the ledger. Are you looking for something in particular from my personal library? A tome by Dr. Johnson, perhaps?"

"A tome? Oh, is that what we are calling it now?" Lizzy said, teasing him.

"Lizzy, close the door and come here."

"No, I shall not the close the door. I know you too well. But I do have something to share. There will be no heir. Not this month, at least," Lizzy said and looked to her husband for his reaction to the news that she had begun her courses.

"Oh, please do not worry about that. We have only been married a month, and there is no hurry."

"What do you mean, 'There is no hurry?' Since when?"

"Well, it *is* only the first month, and I *am* in good health and do not expect to die soon. But if I should become ill in the near future, I shall just have to kill Peter Grayson."

Lizzy gasped. "Will, quickly say a prayer. What an awful thing to say." But she could hardly disguise her amusement. "If you do such a thing, your last months on earth will be spent in gaol."

"Oh, I would not do the deed myself. I would hire it out, possibly to one of those thugees from the Indian subcontinent."

"Shame on you for such thoughts! Besides, you told me that if Peter Grayson predeceases you that your eight-year-old cousin, Malcolm, will become your heir, and that he is an *enfant terrible*."

"He *is* a hellion. But he cannot inherit until he reaches the age of twenty-one. By that time, Georgie will have married and very likely have had a son. So the danger presented by David Grayson may be a short one."

"Really? You are being rather cavalier about something that was of great urgency to you less than two months ago."

"But that is because I have now dedicated my life to siring an heir, and I will continue to avail myself of every opportunity to do so."

"My, my! Such devotion to a cause."

"It is how I am," he said, smiling.

"Well, it is my understanding from my mother that I cannot conceive during my time of month, so I will bid you 'good night,' Mr. Darcy.

"And I shall say 'good night' to you as well. However, you will be the dutiful wife and tell me as soon as your time has passed, so that we might get about the business of producing an heir."

"Friday. Three days hence. But you may sleep with me if you wish."

Darcy jumped out of his chair and was soon kissing Elizabeth with a good deal of passion.

"Will, I just told you…"

"Yes, I know, but please do not ever stop me from kissing you. It is my greatest pleasure."

* * *

Elizabeth and Will returned to Pemberley in mid July. Georgiana's first season had been a huge success, as was Elizabeth's in her role as Mrs. Fitzwilliam Darcy. She had been greeted warmly by her husband's circle of friends, and she was surprised to find that Caroline Bingley Grayson wanted to be her friend. "After all, we are related now, and our properties in Derbyshire are right next to each other," Caroline had told Lizzy on the night of the Thurston ball. "Peter has such fond memories of Pemberley, and he mentions them quite frequently."

Yes, but don't start measuring for the drapes, just yet, Lizzy thought. *I fully intend to produce an heir—and a spare.*

During the ball, Lizzy had ample opportunity to study Mr. and Mrs. Peter Grayson. Caroline was absolutely gorgeous in an ivory gown with embroidered sleeves and waist, but almost her equal in beauty was her husband, who was gorgeously accoutered in the latest fashion and with every curl in his coiffed head in place. Although they spent most of the evening apart, Peter and Caroline would occasionally wave to each other across a crowded room, and though Lizzy found such behavior odd in newlyweds, it seemed that the couple was perfectly content with the arrangement. When Lizzy mentioned it to William, he gave her his "cat that ate the canary" grin, but would make no comment. What exactly did he know that she did not?

* * *

On the first morning after their arrival at Pemberley, Lizzy was greeted with a sun rising on a gorgeous summer day. The gardens were in full bloom, and she roused her husband from a deep sleep so that they might enjoy the coolest part of the day together.

"Will, in March, when I visited with the vicar, he told me that he believed that love could grow in the fertile soil of Pemberley," Lizzy said as they strolled through the gardens, "and he was right. When we married, there was no evidence of a flower on any of these plants, but by the time we left for London, they were already starting to bloom. Now, they are bursting with color and scent, and they enrich our lives. And on or about our first anniversary, we shall have a little cutting to add to our garden." Darcy looked at her, and she nodded.

"Oh, Lizzy, we are truly blessed. Thank you, my dear." And as they walked hand in hand, Darcy whispered to her, "Now that you are with child, I shall not have to kill Peter Grayson. I was not looking forward to it."

Lizzy's mouth fell open, but if she wanted to reprimand him, she would have to catch him, and he quickly ran away and waved to her from the far side of the garden. "Come along, Mrs. Darcy," he shouted.

"You need the exercise. After all, you are exercising for two."

The End

ABOUT THE AUTHOR

Mary Lydon Simonsen combines her love of history and the novels of Jane Austen in writing re-imaginings of Miss Austen's work. She is the author of *Searching for Pemberley* and *The Perfect Bride for Mr. Darcy* which are available in bookstores and on line. Her third *Pride and Prejudice* inspired novel, *A Wife for Mr. Darcy*, will be available in July 2011. Also available, exclusively on-line, is a *Persuasion* re-imagining, *Anne Elliot, A New Beginning*, as well as her modern novel, *The Second Date, Love Italian-American Style*. The author lives in Arizona.

10135270R0

Made in the USA
Lexington, KY
27 June 2011